D0935897

DOMINOES

&
Other Stories
from the Puerto Rican

Jack Agüeros

CURBSTONE PRESS

FIRST EDITION, 1993
Copyright © 1993 by Jack Agüeros
ALL RIGHTS RESERVED

Cover illustration: Chris Thorkelson
Printed in the U.S. on acid-free paper by BookCrafters

"AGUA VIVA," A SCULPTURE BY ALFREDO GONZALEZ,
copyright © 1980, was first published in Revista Chicano-
Riquena, Año VIII, #4.
DOMINOES, copyright ©1992, was first published in Callaloo,
Vol. 15, #4.
SANTOS NEGRON, copyright ©1986, was first published in 1986
in Sombra, Vol. 1, #1.

Curbstone Press is a 501(c)(3) nonprofit literary arts organization
whose operations are supported in part by private donations and
by grants from the ADCO Foundation, the J. Walton Bissell
Foundation, the Connecticut Commission on the Arts, the LEF
Foundation, the Lila Wallace-Reader's Digest Literary
Publishers Marketing Development Program, administered by
the Council of Literary Magazines and Presses, the Andrew W.
Mellon Foundation, the National Endowment for the Arts, and the
Plumsock Fund.

Library of Congress Cataloging-in-Publication Data

Agüeros, Jack, 1934—
    Dominoes & other stories / Jack Agueros. — 1st ed.
        p.   cm.
    ISBN 1-880684-11-X : $14.95
    1. Puerto Ricans—United States—Fiction. I. Title. II. Title:
Dominoes and other stories.
PS3551.G845D66 1993
813'.54—dc20   93-4849

distributed in the U.S. by
InBook, Box 120261, East Haven, CT 06512

CURBSTONE PRESS
321 Jackson Street   Willimantic, CT 06226

CONTENTS

Dominoes   9

Horologist   22

Johnny United   55

Malig; Malig & Sal; Sal.   68

One Sunday Morning   96

Oscar's Story   109

Santos Negron   119

"Agua Viva," A Sculpture
        By Alfredo Gonzalez   140

to my mother
Carmen Agüeros Diaz
who told me stories
and still does

DOMINOES

& Other Stories
from the Puerto Rican

DOMINOES

DOUBLE SIX:
THE BOX OF TEETH

Ebarito liked to hold six dominoes in his left hand. And he wished his hands were larger so that he might span all seven at once. But even Paco with his large hands could not hold seven dominoes.

He tapped the single domino he held in his right hand once on the board. It was a signal that meant he passed. It was irritating to pass at his first turn in the first game.

Paco, sitting to Ebarito's right, laughed a simple "ha," and said nothing.

Tito, the next player, played his domino at a right angle to the double six that Paco had led with. And he also kept another domino spinning at his right hand by periodically snapping his index finger and his thumb.

Wilson, the fourth player liked to lay his dominoes on their sides in one semicircle. He took one and placed it on the board, then tightened the semicircle.

Paco laughed two loud "ha's" and slapped his domino down on the board. When he took his hand away Ebarito could see he would have to pass again since the game was at sixes at both ends.

"*No voy*," he said in Spanish, without tapping his domino.

Paco laughed one "ha."

Tito, playing one and spinning one, said, "Remember, many of one, few of another."

Ebarito took a long drink from his can of beer.

Wilson looked at his little round wall and played a domino. Then he said, "Only three of those."

Paco played and said, "You know how to count, but the game was invented by a mute."

Another round had gone by and Ebarito saw that he was controlling the threes. But it was too late in this game. He had passed twice and might have to pass once more. There was no doubt about it — Paco had the luck and the skill. It was very hard to beat him in a game of dominoes. And especially when he teamed up with Tito — or even worse when he teamed up with Wilson. Luckily today Wilson was Ebarito's partner and so Ebarito had expectations of making a decent showing — perhaps even coming in under the one hundred point handicap that Paco had offered. If Paco had teamed with Wilson, Ebarito could have gotten a handicap of 200 points — but so what — nobody could beat Paco and Wilson, not even with a 250 point handicap. And with a handicap that large there was no purpose to the game. A handicap only meant something if it was the element that wobbled the wheel of fortune.

Ebarito finished his beer. Decided he would not drink another one. None of them drank, why should he? Or maybe they just wouldn't drink with him.

DOUBLE FIVE

Alma leaned on the ledge of her second floor window. With a cushion under her elbows she could sit like this for hours, enjoying the street life. The boys were not yet playing stoop ball. But by the *bodega*, near the empty yard, she could see her uncle Paco playing dominoes with of all people, Ebarito. Most of the men disliked Ebarito. And even though he had a reputation as a good barber the men avoided him. And as he also had a reputation as a lousy domino player it was strange to see him sitting there teamed up with Wilson. Her uncle Paco had told her once, "Ebarito is nothing but a barber and a pretty boy. He can't play dominoes and he's always trying. In the merchant marine we were all barbers."

She had learned the game out of curiosity — she couldn't see what was in it that kept the men sitting there day and night playing and playing. In the summer in the street and in the winter in her kitchen.

She had begged uncle Paco to teach her the game and one Saturday evening, when her old boyfriend Sammy had stood her up, he took the dominoes out and said, "Sit down." He was a man like that — couldn't express too many things and yet he was smart. For twenty years he sailed around the world visiting many interesting places, reading when he was not playing. But he just didn't talk very much.

Dominoes seemed to Alma a ridiculous game. Whoever got the double six played first if you were just starting. Once you played the first game whoever won started the next game. Then it was just a matter of following the numbers. Your opponent put down a six, you played a six. Your opponent put down a two, you put down a two. If you didn't have something you passed. But her uncle said it wasn't like that at all. He said there was strategy. If you had a two-five and a four-five and you could play a five, which one would you play? Well, that was strategy. You looked over the board, you counted all the fours, you counted all the twos, you looked at your own hand, and you decided which one to play. That wasn't luck, that was skill. That was how you controlled the game.

But Alma didn't like the game — if she wanted to kill time she preferred looking out the window, and in the winter she liked cards now and then — especially a game called "Casino." For the moment she was more interested in her new boyfriend PeeWee. She was hoping he would come over from 112th Street, where he lived near Third Avenue. And perhaps he would invite her for a walk in Central Park or better still, to a movie. She hadn't been to a movie in a few weeks, and the Star Theater on 107th and Lexington was playing two good films. But PeeWee did not come around the corner.

DOUBLE FOUR

Paco shifted his weight on the milk crate he was siting on.

Ebarito played one of his threes.

Tito knocked on the board, close to where his domino was spinning.

"Oh, oh, somebody's got no threes or sixes," said Wilson.

Ebarito said, "I believe Paco said this was a game invented by a mute."

Paco slapped down his domino with great force, and when he removed his ham sized hand he said, "*Lo tranque*. I locked it at sixes — let's go, count up."

Tito took everyone's dominoes and counted forty two points, then turned them all face down.

Paco mixed the dominoes driving his left hand clockwise, and his right hand counterclockwise, slightly out of synchronization.

Tito said, "I like a hand where I have four of something and they don't come out until the second or third play."

"Take your dominoes," said Paco leaving his hands at the side of the board. This meant he would take last — take whatever remained. It was like a boxer dropping his gloves to his sides and daring his opponent to hit him.

Ebarito took his seven, skipping around hoping to get a better selection. But he was feeling worse and worse. He had no business in this foursome. This was strictly a losing proposition for him. His game was women; the barber shop. His hand was terrible, three doubles. *"La caja de muerto,"* the dead man's box, meaning the double blank, and *"La caja de dientes,"* meaning the box of teeth, or the double six, and the double three. This was going to be another painful and embarrassing loss. He could see that he would lose by 250 points — the 100 point handicap would be just another humiliation.

"No voy," said Tito furiously spinning his domino.

"Already?" said Wilson.

By the next play Ebarito had to pass and he struck his domino down with a hard sharp blow — like an angry gaveling. And he wished it were a nail that he could drive through the board and into the ground. He knew he was going to lose, knew he had but one recourse now — to lose gracefully — be a good sport — offer to buy everyone a beer, a cigar or a drink — say the obvious out loud — "You are too good for me" — but Goddammit he couldn't do it — it stuck in his craw like a thing he could not swallow, could not spit.

DOUBLE THREE

Of all the sounds on the street the sharp blow of a domino on a wooden board caught Alma's attention. It was a sound she had heard many times before, and which she disliked. When she looked over at the game Ebarito looked angry, but she still couldn't see Paco's face. She could see Wilson, whom she didn't like although she had known him all her life. He was her uncle's best friend. A master domino player and a very hard man. He believed in fate. "Men who are real men can live their lives anyway they like — because their destiny is clear. To be a *macho* is the destiny. The trouble for you Alma is that you fool around with men who are not *machos*," he had told her once in her kitchen. "And for a woman, Wilson, what is the fate for a woman?" "I don't know," he had answered, "I don't know anything about women. For women I recommend an *espiritista* and the church. One will tell you the future and the other will console you about it. But I'm not sure which does what."

After that pronouncement both Wilson and Paco had broken into very heavy prolonged laughter. Tito was not like that. He was kinder and he talked more, but he was not as strong as they were. They could make him do the opposite of what he believed. But they genuinely liked him — not because they influenced him, but because they seemed to enjoy his company — he was what they were not — social and friendly, fun loving and relaxed. But he had not left Puerto Rico to join the merchant marine when he was sixteen — like Wilson or Paco. They were just *jibaro* kids — country boys suddenly with mean men and dangerous work and thirty years at sea always looking to see who was standing behind you. Tito had steady legs, like a man used to walking on the earth. Wilson and Paco had a strange gait, always waiting for the sea to pitch!

DOUBLE TWO

Tito played and was talking. "You know my father used to say when we were watching the baseball games — 'The ball is round, son, the game is not over until the last out.' But in dominoes, especially in double-six, the game is over as soon as you get your hand. Isn't it?"

Paco grimaced. He believed in skill.

"I know, I know, the game was invented by a mute. But I can't be like you Paco — I can't sit through a whole game and not say a word — to me part of this game is talking — about this about that."

"Oh yeah — some people even say that that is your strategy as a team. You yak yak to distract them while Paco . . ." Ebarito let his voice trail off.

"While Paco what?" asked Tito and Wilson at the same time.

"Yeah, while Paco what, little barber?" asked Paco.

"Something the matter with being a barber?" asked Ebarito while playing his double six.

Paco stared at the board.

"Apparently barbers can't count," said Paco.

"Right," said Tito, the domino perfectly still under his right index finger, "you passed on six before — it's called reneging."

"You calling me a cheater?" asked Ebarito standing up.

"No," said Paco, "but then you better admit you can't count."

"Perhaps your mother can't count," said Ebarito. And in the moment that his words were being formed in his mouth he bent over, picked up the metal milk crate he had been sitting on and swung it at Paco's head.

Paco was already rising, his straightening legs upending the board, the dominoes scattering, and with his left arm he grabbed the milk crate and pushed it back into Ebarito's chest. And Ebarito went backward, losing his balance, down. And Paco was on top of him, both massive hands tightly around Ebarito's throat.

Tito went to break it up, but Wilson pulled him by the arm, and hissed, "Fuck the pretty boy barber," and Tito just stopped, as if Wilson's venom had paralyzed him.

Then Paco started to lift Ebarito's head and strike it against the sidewalk at the same time that he tightened his hands ever more around his neck. Ebarito reached into his jacket and pulled out the long thin trimming scissor with the loop that cradles the pinky and adds balance and control to the tool. He began to drive the scissor into Paco's rib cage with a circular motion from the elbow, for the rest of his arm was immobilized by Paco's knee.

"They are killing each other," gasped Tito to Wilson who was still holding him.

DOUBLE ONE

Alma broke out of a reverie to see PeeWee across the street calling her and yelling and pointing over to the vacant lot. When Alma looked she let go a scream and yelled, "Paco, Paco, stop it, stop it, Wilson stop them. Tito for God's sake do something. PeeWee call the police." And she screamed again. But no one moved.

She screamed again, her hands covering her ears as if she could not tolerate her own penetrating wail. And then she turned into the apartment. When she was no longer visible in the window PeeWee came to life again, for he had been more startled by the screaming than by the fight. The screaming turned the fight into something more serious than he had at first thought.

He looked in two directions trying to remember where the nearest phone was. And then he headed for the corner drugstore, before he could see Alma come screaming out of her hallway like a train out of a tunnel onto the street.

Wilson still held Tito's arm in a vice-like grip. "They are *machos,*" said Wilson seeming to speak through clenched teeth, "they know what they want."

But at the sight of Alma pulling at Paco, Tito broke loose and kicked the scissor from Ebarito's hand and pulled at Paco too.

Paco stood up thinking Ebarito was dead. He took a few staggering steps and then found his balance, and began walking off in no particular direction. But his left rib cage looked like a colander with blood pouring out of twelve scissor holes, some spurting, some just trickling down over the already forming clots. And when he reached the fire hydrant Paco crumbled down into a pile like a pneumatic tire that had a blow out.

He was dead.

He was dead before he fell.

He was dead even before he stood up and walked.

The body had its habits and in a man who spoke very little, his body had spoken last — it had refused to die where fate had ordained — he didn't want to be near Ebarito. Death wanted him there, but he would go here.

Alma in tears, in terror and hysteria was on her knees crying and screaming next to the body of the wrong man, for it was inconceivable to her that Ebarito could be alive and her uncle dead. She screamed over the bloody head, face and body of Ebarito, "You killed him, you let him be killed, you killers." She screamed at everyone. She screamed at no one.

DOUBLE BLANK
THE DEAD MAN'S BOX

Ebarito awoke. Pain played over his body head to throat to arm. And he realized he had his eyes closed.

He tried to open his eyes and found it difficult to do. He could not turn his head and his neck seemed very stiff. As he tried to feel his body beyond the pain he discovered that he could not lift his head, and while he did not seem to be tied down, he couldn't shift his weight at all. He could curl his fingers and wiggle his toes. His tongue felt huge in his mouth: as if he had a washcloth stuffed there rather than a tongue. His left arm was more mobile but he could only raise it somewhat. He tried to open his eyes again.

And when he opened them everything seemed to be clouded and out of focus. And there was nothing but white to see, but there was the unmistakable smell of hospital — like there was the unmistakable smell of barbershop, of dentist, of laundry.

Then he heard a squeaky wheel, footsteps, and heard someone speaking. The doctor was asking, "Do you understand English? — Do you speak English? English?"

Painfully he tried to shake his head yes, as he could not find his voice. He could not move the wash rag in his mouth, nor spit it out. And he could not shake his head either.

The doctor was saying, "Lucky boy you are to be alive — your skull was cracked — do you remember?"

"No," said the doctor, "you can't speak — he wrecked your trachea, larynx? — you know — voice box? Adam's apple? With a little oxygen deprivation — maybe asphyxia. Drove your cricoid up against the 7th in the neck — you understand? You have cracks in your trachea. Severe damage to the vocal cords from bone and cartilage pushing up against them, tearing through them. You may never be able to speak — maybe growl. I did some marvelous work in there — you understand — *vida* — life? Serious concussion, on your *cabeza* — you know — head, *cabeza*? One eye is fine — a matter of a few days, maybe two weeks and we will know the whole story on the eyes. There is a little infection there now — *infección,* you know?"

Ebarito tried to point to his mouth, but his left arm was manacled to the bed.

HOROLOGIST

(By Appointment Only)

WEDNESDAY

Without turning his head he felt a person approach and look into the window behind him. A male. Whether there was actually a physical clue like a small dimming of the light coming over his shoulder, or whether it was some slight motion reflected in one of the three magnifying lenses he wore attached to his working eyeglasses, he couldn't say, but he always knew when anyone was behind him, whenever anyone looked into the store window and whenever they moved away. His partner, Mr. Livrehomme, had arranged the store.

"This way, Mr. Vazquez," Livrehomme never called him by his first name Maximiliano or Max. Livrehomme didn't like that American instant familiarity where people who just met you called you Max and Joe as if they had known you forever — "This way, Mr. Vazquez, they can entertain themselves without coming in and actually standing over your shoulder. We'll put the workbench near the window. People always want to watch others at work. Especially at jobs they know nothing about and consider unusual and interesting. So they'll walk by, look in the window, and they won't bother you."

Greenwich Avenue in New York is one of the shopping streets of Greenwich Village, but mercifully they were down at the quieter end of it, near Eighth Avenue, where pedestrian flow tapers off substantially. Still, Vazquez could feel many people stopping and looking over his shoulder as he worked. At first it had been a great distraction. Every peeker made him stop and turn around. Then he and Livrehomme had installed a mirror and all he had to do was look up into the mirror to see who was watching him from the street.

That was when they opened the store here, workshop more than store, fifteen years ago. Now he never looked in the mirror, never turned around. Years ago, he realized that whenever he looked into the mirror it was because someone was approaching the window. It occurred to him that he was ahead of the mirror. And if he was ahead of the mirror in this way, could he be ahead of the mirror in other ways? If he could sense the people before seeing them in the mirror, perhaps he could sense other things as well. And he began guessing whether they were male or female, tall or short, fat or skinny, young or old, and then he would look in the mirror to confirm his guess. He had gotten so good at guessing that he rarely glanced at the mirror for confirmation.

Vazquez knew that the person watching him was a young man, medium stature, maybe his own height

5'9" give or take a half inch. But his attention turned to his timer, which was about to go off, signalling him to remove a number of brass wheels he was soaking in an ammoniated soap solution. Village stores had been hit with a number of armed robberies in the recent past and as Vazquez removed his brass wheels and rinsed them in warm water washing off both the grime and the cleansing solution, he looked up in the mirror to see the face of the young man. Was it the face of a young robber, "casing the joint" as they used to say on the old radio programs? Well, if he looked around he would see that there wasn't anything really to rob. Not cash, and only a real expert would know anything about the many clocks or where to sell them.

Then again there was an article about a major clock robbery in the Bulletin just recently. Two in fact. Clock thefts from a house, and clock thefts from a dealer in California. And every time there was an auction at Southeby's and clock prices skyrocketed, that made things worrisome.

But it was always the unscrupulous who made things terrible. Not the thieves. The thieves only operated because the unscrupulous paid for stolen merchandise. They were the truly corrupt and the corrupters. No buyers of stolen property, no thieves.

And when the timer went off the young man walked away, away toward Eighth Avenue.

What do you call it when you always anticipate your timer by a few seconds? Mr. Livrehomme used to say in class that men and women who became horologists had a clock in them that sought out other clocks; a clock in them that could be heard in their own ears; that day or night they always knew the approximate time. "Why not the real time or the exact time?" some student would always ask. And Livrehomme would always reply, with an enigmatic smile on his lips, "Because there is no such thing, there is only approximate time, relative time." And he would go on to another subject.

THURSDAY

Vazquez was placing the mechanism for a long case clock up on the workhorse when he realized that something was happening across the street. The mirror was tilted so that he could see out about half way across the street on Greenwich, and then only at the pavement tar with its double yellow line. Through the window he saw a figure crossing the street and coming toward the store. The young man again.

Vazquez didn't want to be distracted. Mounting the case on the horse was a maneuver that required care. The clock work had to sit up well balanced so it wouldn't topple over, and level, so that the pendulum would swing properly. He looked for the wooden shims and the spirit level and worked the wood around under the brass plates until he was satisfied that he had a level clockwork in two directions. Next he had to attach the great weights to the chains, and finally hang the pendulum which was very beautiful.

This clock was a beautiful clock in a beautiful case. It was a historic clock, early American, 18th Century, perhaps pre-revolution, made in Pennsylvania. One of the earliest clocks completely made in the colonies. But the museum and its curators had too high an opinion of the piece and it was terribly overestimated in dollar value as well.

Vazquez felt the mechanism was now well balanced, but the young man was not to be seen on either side of Greenwich Avenue.

The robberies were something to worry about. Hadn't he gotten a police circular warning about a stick-up team? But that circular talked about a young woman who would enter the store first, then a man would come in later. And they were after cash, they never took merchandise.

FRIDAY

The Old Dutch Master's Club was located in midtown, near the Harvard Club. Its official name was the Lowlands Club, but only out of towners ever called it by that name. They wanted Vazquez to inspect a clock and offer an estimate for restoration. The Old Dutch Masters considered their clock an heirloom.

"An important clock," said the President of the club, "important in the history of our great city."

The clock was hung high on a wall in the club's main room, not far from a fireplace. They took it down clumsily, two kitchen employees teetering on chairs instead of using a stable ladder. Vazquez cautioned them to get adequate ladders before putting it back, and the club president looked irritated. Vazquez opened the clock, noticing the soot on one side of the case, and candle wax residue all over the case as he looked in. He opened the back, removed the pendulum, and flashed his penlight into the case. He didn't like what he saw. Heavy black incrustation everywhere. Oily brass plates. Thin, oily brass plates. Bad signs.

Vazquez asked the President when it had last been attended to, and when it had stopped.

"We had a member of the club who repaired clocks as a hobby, and he regularly oiled it and set it going," said the President who was bothered by this inspection. "It's truly a beautiful clock isn't it?"

Vazquez didn't agree, didn't comment at all, and then irritated the Dutch Masters more by telling them that he doubted if the clock was a very good timekeeper.

"How could you know that?" demanded the President of the club. "We haven't seen it working in about ten years."

"When I look inside I see certain clues. I get a first impression, but I'll give you a written statement of my findings and opinions, after a full examination."

"Do you say we shouldn't bother to fix it?" asked the President with an incredulous tone in his voice. "We had a horologist here before you who told us the clock was worth at least $30,000."

"Well," said Vazquez, taking a long time between his "well" and his next words, "have him restore it for you."

"You have higher recommendations," added another man, apparently a member of the committee on the clock.

The President looked flustered, and the other man asked sharply, "In your opinion, is the clock worth $30,000, if it's not a good timekeeper?"

Vazquez didn't like to think about the worth of clocks in dollar terms. "I don't appraise clocks, I don't buy or sell clocks. But if you respect the clock, or it has special meaning to you, then the clock is priceless, isn't it? And if we can get it to work at all..."

The committee of three men squirmed in their seats.

"You mean to tell us that it may not work at all?"

"It'll work. But you may have to set the time every two weeks."

"Twice a week! The appraiser told us it was a thirty day clock!"

"I said every two weeks. A hundred and fifty years ago when this clock was probably made..."

"You mean three hundred and fifty years ago," shot the President of the club. "That's what we were told."

The committee excused Vazquez, curtly thanking him for coming by. Vazquez went down to the main club room and looked at the clock again. It was a type of long case clock, nearly as long as a grandmother clock, but it had been designed to hang on a wall, rather than to stand freely. That suggested to Vazquez that it probably had been commissioned for a particular wall — perhaps a public building in a small town in Holland. It had good cabinetwork, the cabinet better than the clockwork. The face was uninteresting, with easy to read numbers and so-so hands. The innards he knew were European but not French. Although the works were of brass, they were very thin and didn't have the fine details of French clock-making like an oil sink. It probably had been made in some obscure workshop in Holland. And it was an example of low quality clock work, a mediocre work stuck in a much better quality cabinet. That happened and so did the opposite, very fine clockwork stuck in a so-so box.

Vazquez could guess who had given the appraisal. That was a job he never wanted. If the clock meant something in the history of the club, if it meant something to the members, a linkage with their past and the humble man who had brought the clock to America, why didn't that make it worth setting to go again? Why couldn't they be proud that at its age it could still be made to work at all?

He paused to look at it again from the door. It was hung too high on the wall, and looked awkward and out of proportion. Was it worth $300, let alone $30,000? Why did appraisers over-value, over-age?

It didn't matter to Vazquez, he would like to get it going. It deserved to be respected, to be restored, because if Vazquez understood one thing it was "sentimental value."

SATURDAY

The morning had been wonderfully quiet. He had opened the shop up at 10 p.m. as usual. It had been raining all morning and not one person had paused at the window, and before he knew it, it was 2:30 p.m. The phone rang sometime after that and it was the Old Dutch Master's Club.

"Max?"

"Mr. Vazquez speaking. Who is this, please?"

"This is Pete VanBramer, Max. We want you to fix the clock. We understand that you work with Livrehomme, and the committee wanted the assurance that it was so. Is it?"

"We have been partners for fifteen years and we discuss all the clocks together before we remove them from their cases. We keep a log of what we find, and what we do. We give you a copy for your files when we return your clock, and we keep one in our files."

"Good. And another thing, Max. We consider this a restoration. We don't want parts changed or fake things stuck in there. You know what I mean?"

"Mr. VanBramer, we do only restorations."

"Call me Pete, Max. We're not trying to hurt your feelings, but the committee has a right to make sure of these things. Now, how fast can we get the clock back?"

"Fast?"

"Yeah. Will it be a cupala weeks, or what?"

"Six to seven months more likely."

"What? Are you that backlogged? Well, look Max, we'll pay a little more for expediting, if you like."

"Mr. VanBramer, I believe your President said the clock hadn't been working for ten years. Six or seven months will pass relatively quickly. I'll be by to pick up the clock on Monday. Please arrange to have two good six foot ladders. Thank you and goodbye."

MONDAY

Livrehomme laughed. "I think you were easy on them. I can see from here you will have great difficulty with three of these pivots. You will have to bush them. The plates are so thin, if you don't bush them they'll be elliptical again in no time. And I wonder about the quality of the brass, not much copper in the plates. Look at the pivots: elliptical."

Livrehomme moved over so that Vazquez could get his head closer to the case. Vazquez swung two of the magnifying lenses into place in front of his eyeglasses and peeked into the case. "Yes. They're eggs. I don't think there are any broken teeth or wheels. By the way they said they didn't want any fake stuff."

They laughed together.

"What do you think they had in mind?" asked Livrehomme.

"I'm sure they hadn't the slightest idea. They think we take out good pieces and put cheap pieces back in, I guess."

"I didn't see any fragments on the floor of the case, did you?" asked Livrehomme.

Vazquez took his penlight and shined it into the case bottom. "Nothing down there but dust."

"A good cleaning and three new pivots, at least. The clock is filthy. You'll hope the arbors don't have flat sides. If they do, then you'll have real restoration questions. They look too thin to work on. Then you'll have to machine new parts."

"When they took the clock down so I could inspect it, I noticed different gradations of color on the wall. And the outline of the clock repeated. You could barely see it from up close. It's the old story, each time they wound it they moved it over just a bit. Over the years they took it way out of plumb, and I'm sure that's why the pivots are out of round. Everything pulling in this one direction."

"Sure. So their well meaning member took it down, obviously oiled it again and again, set it back up level, and it would work for a while. Until they slowly moved it again. Psst! Pivots out of round, arbors with flat sides. When will you start work on it?"

"Four weeks, at least. I just got the museum clock up on the horse on Thursday and I'm going to try and get it going tomorrow. By the way, I think the curator got us this job with the Old Dutch Masters. He told them this clock was worth $30,000 dollars."

"No. No curator gives appraisals now. It was our friend Hughard the dealer, and I'm sure they loved that figure."

"Yes, they did but they didn't like it when I told them it might not keep good time. I thought we wouldn't get the job."

"We are doing very good work on very good clocks. You didn't have to take this job."

"Something about the clock. I imagined an old immigrant Dutchman, running from the Germans, carrying his special clock to America. You know? You know Mr. Livrehomme?"

"Yes, I know, Mr. Vazquez, I know you make up good stories for all your clocks. You owe it to this man you never met, isn't that what you figure?"

"Sort of," answered Vazquez.

"Then you know what, Mr. Vazquez, there's a good chance that it might keep good time. Consider bushing all the pivots. There aren't that many wheels. And when you remount it on the wall, build in two level stop blocks so the clock can't be moved out of plumb."

And then they looked at the clock and didn't speak for awhile, like people who stare into a fireplace, gripped by the dance of the flames while their own thoughts fly.

"I've been thinking about talking to that woman who has the shop uptown. She's an old student of mine and she has a good apprentice. If we all came together we could have a real atelier. Reduce overhead and become even more picky." Livrehomme started laughing. "Seriously, there's now room in New York for a real old world atelier — I think maybe there is even room for us to manufacture some special clocks in limited editions. Three different clocks. Only ten of each. How would you like that? We could become really picky. This dutch clock could be prepared by an apprentice while you and I could design clocks, supervise production, and especially control quality. I know a man who's an excellent cabinet maker."

"I'm not sure I'd like that. I like to take a clock apart down to the last pin and then put it all back together again. I hate production lines. I hate mass production. On the other hand I like the idea of being picky. Maybe we can have the owners fill out an application with a section for a statement, 'I want this clock repaired because...'" Then Vazquez laughed, and Livrehomme laughed more.

TUESDAY

When Vazquez first became interested in clocks, he liked faces. Sometimes he also liked the cases. As he learned more about clocks, he came to love the inner works and to be very indifferent about face dials and cabinet work. Livrehomme had said at one of Vazquez's first classes, "You can form no opinion of a clock from the outside." Sometimes he would say it another way: "A clock is not the case."

Vazquez looked at it differently. When a man bothered to make a fine clock work, he was likely to put a handsome face on it, and to want it in a fine cabinet. But Livrehomme was right, a fine face and a fine cabinet could be the marks of a fine clock, but unscrupulous clock men made what are called "marriages" in the trade. He himself had found a fine french clock work in a very strange white metal cabinet. The clock looked as if it had been taken from some other cabinet and stuck into the metal one. Some dealers would have no compunction about passing such a marriage off as an original clock. Caveat emptor! A decent dealer would tell you it was suspected of being a marriage, and a good dealer would tell you it was probably a marriage and let you decide if you still wanted it. Some people collected "marriages," and didn't mind any price at all for one.

But this Pennsylvania clock was definitely very special. This clock had been made by one man, works and case. One gifted man from Pennsylvania with a vision and two skills. Clock and cabinet making. One man had been responsible for this fine work. Every detail of it conceived and executed by one demanding artisan. Maybe the museum is right, this Pennsylvania clock is worth $400,000.

"Now all I have to do is make it go," said Vazquez out loud. Then he bent down and gave the pendulum a little push. The clock tick-tocked, tick-tocked, tick-tocked, and stopped.

Vazquez felt the young man staring through the window. The thought that maybe the young man knew the dollar value of the clock and wanted to steal it raced through his mind. But as Vazquez looked for a screwdriver to adjust the escapement, the man walked away from the window.

Good clocks always behaved in the same way. They would go for a little and then stop. Like a person resenting surgery, the clock needed to make a statement to its restorer. This moment, the moment of setting the beat always made him sad, because it was essentially the end of his work. He had grown accustomed to seeing the fine clock and its cabinet day after day and soon he would have to go to the museum to see his old friend. He was about to loosen a screw to adjust the crutch and pallets when the door bell rang. It gave him a start.

The young man presented a beautifully designed card in bright black raised thermofaxed letters that said:

GG Productions
Film & Video Studios
180 West Street
Tribeca, NY 10011

Gary Garcia
President

FAX: 1 - 212 - FILMDEO

There was a drawing of a piece of film reeling out from the screen of a television.

"What can I do for you, Mr. Garcia?"

"You can call me Gary, Mister...? Do you have a card?"

Vazquez searched in his pockets and found none. He went to his workbench and couldn't find one there either. Then he went to the desk and in the upper right hand drawer he found a whole stack of cards, took one from the middle.

Garcia looked at the card.

Horologist
(By Appointment Only)
Mr. Maximiliano Vazquez
NAWCC # 3757
(212) 243-2270

There was no drawing. Garcia read it out loud. "Horologist. by appointment only. Mr. Maximiliano Vazquez. It's perfect Max. I've come to see you because I'm going to make you famous."

"Goodbye Mr. Garcia. I'm very busy right now setting a clock."

"Look, I only need a few minutes of your time."

"I have no minutes for you. Good bye."

"Can I make an appointment? I'll call you. I'll call you tomorrow for an appointment. I'm sorry I interrupted you Max. I'll call you tomorrow. Sorry. Bye."

Vazquez locked the door, took his screwdriver and loosened a retaining screw. Then he shifted the pivot about 1/64th of an inch, which actually pulled the pallets up just a bit on the escape wheel. Then he tightened the retaining screw, took the level and read all four sides of the horse, and gave the pendulum a shove. The clock tick-tocked, tick-tocked, but Vazquez did not like the sound. It wasn't robust, it wasn't balanced. He stopped the pendulum, and loosened the retaining screw again and again moved the pivot, but only a hair, and quickly tightened the screw, took the level all around again, shoved the pendulum. He listened with his ear close to the works. The sound was better. He looked at his wall clock and wrote the time down. It sounded right now. He felt it was going to go on.

WEDNESDAY

The phone rang but he hesitated. Then he picked it up and was relieved to hear Mr. Livrehomme.

"Mr. Vazquez, a man in Sheepshead Bay in Brooklyn bought an old restaurant. In its heyday it was well known for its cheesecake and it had a big reputation as a sea food house. The man who owns it now found a clock in the attic and he wants me to go and look at it. Swears it's an antique."

"Are you?"

"He wouldn't take no for an answer. I told him I would have to charge him $500 for going out there. He said 'fine' without hesitating. What can I do?"

"Go see the clock. But forget about the cheesecake. It's probably been in the attic too."

"I'm taking a cab now, and I'll see you this afternoon."

Mr. Vazquez looked at the Pennsylvania clock and he looked at his wall clock. The Pennsylvania was now four minutes fast. He stopped the pendulum, turned the knurled screw four full times to the left, which lowered the pendulum's bob just a bit. He rolled the hands to the same time as his wall clock, and taking the level all around, nudged the pendulum. When he entered what he had done in the log, he began to look at his job tickets to see what clock was next, but the phone rang again.

"Mr. Vazquez speaking."

"Mr. Vazquez, this is Mr. Garcia. I would like to make an appointment with you. I know I started off on the wrong foot. And I want to correct it. May I take you to lunch? Pick a day."

"Mr. Garcia why don't you just tell me what you'd like over the phone."

"I want to make a one hour program about you as a horologist. I looked it up. I also now know what NAWCC stands for and that you are an old member. And I joined and I went to the library and looked at a copy of the Bulletin. But let me rewind. I'm trying to do a series of between 13 and 26 half hour programs that explore unusual occupations and minority people who not only work in those occupations, but are masters or experts in them. I have, just one example, a Puerto Rican who repairs antique radios. English, American, German or Italian. There isn't a radio that he can't repair. And when I say repair, I mean he can make the radio play. No matter what year it's from. So now. Fast forward. Each program goes like this. It's a mixture of history of the subject. Like clocks. Then it's your biography. How you got in. Then it takes a real look at restoring a clock. Whatever that is — I don't know yet. All the time we use a real classy background music. It's in there, down there, you hear it but not intrusive. A mellow voiced narrator. Sonorous voice. A wow voice. This costs you nothing. In fact. Rewind. I pay you for being on camera, I pay you for time lost while we do it, and you get a small residual right in the video. Now. Quick cut, Mr. Vazquez. This is not schlock video or amateur night. I bring you press clips, I bring you demo reels. I'm talking respect for craft. Creating interest in the history of clocks. Educating people. We do excellent photography. Mr. Vazquez. We are craftsmen like you. Dedicated to our craft. Only the super. Excellence, excellence, excellence. Let me take you to lunch. And I'll answer all your questions. Do you see..."

"Mr. Garcia, call me tomorrow about this time. I'll see if I have an open hour for you."

"Thank you very much Mr. Vazquez."

When Vazquez hung up the phone he looked out the window for a while and it occurred to him that Mr. Garcia had been carrying a still camera when he came into the shop, and that probably Mr. Garcia had been taking pictures of the store and maybe even of himself in it. From across the street. Outrageous!!!

The phone rang and Vazquez took it on the first ring.

"Hello!"

"Mr. Vazquez?"

"Yes."

"It's Mr. Livrehomme — what's the matter?"

"Oh, sorry Mr. Livrehomme. Some kid just put me in a bad mood. Wants to put me on television. Me on television, you in the cheesecake attic. It's our day for nuts."

"There are people in America who have so much money Mr. Vazquez, that they don't know what to do with it. I'm on my way with a Seth Thomas school clock that isn't even an antique. But he wants me to repair it and will give me $1,500 to do it. You figure it out."

"You told him you could get him one in mint condition for a third of that?"

"Yes. I told him. But he said, 'This one was in the attic here. It's different. It's in my family now.' What am I supposed to say after that? He reminded me of you."

Livrehomme laughed and Vazquez laughed more.

THURSDAY

"Max? This is Pete. Pete VanBramer. How's our clock doing?"

"Mr. VanBramer your clock is looking fine where it's mounted."

"How's the work going?"

"Mr. VanBramer, no work is going. I let the clock sit here for at least thirty days before anything happens. It has to get used to our shop. Sometimes old cases develop cracks in a new room, or old cracks badly repaired open up again."

"You mean you haven't done anything to it Max?"

"I inspected it more thoroughly than at your club. Mr. Livrehomme and I consulted on the clock, and I inspect the case every morning."

"You haven't done anything to it!"

"I'm getting to know your clock, and I finished my report and drawing."

"Listen Max, I don't want you to get to know my clock. I don't want any reports or drawings whatever they are. I want it repaired! I fought with my president to hire you. He hated you. I'm gonna look bad if this doesn't get done fast, do you understand? I wanna be the next president of the Dutch Masters. Max, this is important to me. Do you understand?"

"Mr. VanBramer..."

"Damn it Max, call me Pete! This 'Mr. VanBramer' is making me crazy!...Max? Max? Are you there? Max, say something!"

"Mr. VanBramer, I am here, but I don't know what to say. If you want I will bring the clock back immediately, and you can have someone else do the restoration."

"Max, Max, you want me kicked out of my club? They'll kill me if you bring that thing back! Max, I had a gut feeling you were the right guy for this job. How can you let me down like this?"

"Mr. VanBramer, I want to restore the clock, but it has to be done correctly."

"Correctly means you just let it sit there for a month?"

"Yes, Mr. VanBramer. It's one of our procedures. Plus every clock has to wait its turn."

There was a long silence, and Vazquez wished he could hang up.

"Look, Max, my president said all you clock guys were like old codgers even if you weren't old. What's the harm in moving our clock up on your agenda?"

"Wouldn't be fair to others, and it wouldn't be fair to you. We have to watch that case. We built a reputation because we do things right. No one complains about our restorations Mr. VanBramer. But if you want to take it elsewhere, that is your prerogative."

"I wanted it chiming before our election. People will hear it and say Pete VanBramer got it repaired. Max, you gotta do it. We'll pay you double. I'll match the fee out of my own pocket. Money's not a problem."

"You're right Mr. VanBramer. Money is not a problem. The problem is time. Get another restorer and call me. I'll cooperate fully with whoever you get. Goodbye!"

FRIDAY

When Vazquez arrived the store smelled of coffee. Livrehomme had made a pot of espresso and wearing the lab coat he liked to wear while working on clocks, had the works of the Seth Thomas on his work table.

"I didn't know you were so eager to work on that Seth Thomas," said Vazquez sipping his straight black coffee.

"This is not eagerness. This is fear of the kind of man who is going to call me every day. You think VanBramer is bad? This man told me that he wants three weeks notice before the clock is ready so he can organize a homecoming and installation party. He's going to invite 1500 people. And next to the clock he's going to install a brass plaque that says, 'Seth Thomas, American School House Clock, circa 19 something.' He wants me to date it for him exactly."

"1500 people and an unveiling ceremony! And a sign as if it were a museum display. Isn't he embarrassed about the age? Is it dated in the case?"

"I didn't find the usual code. I'll look it up later in Tran Duy Ly's book, but I'm putting it between 1938 and 1942. It's in very good condition, but the winding spring is slipping on the arbor. By the way I forgot to tell you, the owner wanted me to put chimes in. I refused, thinking I had found a way out of servicing his clock, but after some grumbling he said forget the chimes but he insisted that I fix it. I told him I'd get him a really beautiful grandfather clock, for the entrance to the dining room for less money than he would pay me to repair the Seth Thomas, but he didn't like that idea. I'll give this a bath, work on the winding arbor. Maybe I reassemble it today. What about you?"

"The Pennsylvania is keeping good time on the horse. Today I'll put it back in the case and if it's still on time 30 days from now, it'll be ready to go back to the museum. I want to see it keep time until it's completely unwound. They'll be happy to get it a month from now. I'll be sad. But I can always pay four bucks and visit it at the Colonial Gallery of the museum."

"You forget that they gave you a complimentary membership. Then?"

"Then I have the collector's clock. The 19th Century French with the strange bell on top. It's so strange I like it. And there's the two from our friend Hughard the dealer. And don't forget I have to go up to that town up state to give an estimate on the street clock. If they accept the estimate — no, forget that. I have to figure out if I can restore it up there or if I have to figure out how to ship it down here, and whether they'll pay for that. I'll bet you I wind up going up there a couple of times."

"Why don't you hold off on Hughard. He has time. Get rid of the Old Dutch Masters."

"You think Hughard won't mind?"

"Give him a call. I'm sure he'll say it's OK."

"Then there's the kid who says he going to make me famous."

"What about him?"

"Nothing about him. Plenty about me. I don't want to be famous. I don't want to be on television."

"Mr. Vazquez, I think it would be good to have a program on clock restoration on television. Maybe people will get an appreciation of why we don't, can't, work fast fast fast. And the kinds of problems we come up against."

"Maybe you should do it."

"He wants a Puerto Rican."

"I know. I'm having lunch with him tomorrow."

"Where are you going?"

"He wanted to take me to a place owned by movie stars in Soho. I said I wanted pizza at John's on Bleecker Street."

"So enjoy your lunch, and keep an open mind. You don't have to decide tomorrow."

SATURDAY

Vazquez arrived at John's a little early. He had talked to Hughard yesterday and Hughard had agreed to wait for his clocks, so Vazquez had already taken the Dutch clock from its case, had inspected it carefully, made notes, and a drawing that he always made of the plates and wheels. By putting back pressure on the wheels he could see three arbors waddling in their pivots, instead of tightly and freely turning. And he could already clearly see one arbor with a flat side. That meant he had to get a new arbor made by his machinist, and perhaps also a new wheel cut. He anticipated VanBramer's voice echoing in his ear, "no fake stuff." But it was either a new arbor or a clock that would never keep time properly. So, let VanBramer decide on Monday.

Garcia was now late and Vazquez relished the thought that Garcia would never arrive, and if he missed this lunch, Vazquez need never speak to him again.

But Garcia arrived, twenty minutes late, dragging a luggage cart squatting under three boxes.

"Mr. Vazquez I had to come over here earlier this week to make special arrangements. Luckily, they don't have much of a lunch crowd on Saturdays, so they set aside this booth for us where I have outlets below. Don't these wooden booths remind you of church pews?"

"Best pizza in New York I think."

"Yeah, you're right, but is it a sin to sit on cushions?"

Vazquez smiled as Garcia began unpacking his three boxes and uncoiling a mass of cables.

"Do you want to order — this takes me a few minutes," said Garcia hauling a small color monitor onto the table.

"Pepperoni, mushrooms, anchovies," answered Vazquez detecting a grimace on Garcia's face at the word "anchovies."

"To drink?"

"A glass of wine, and if you don't mind, I would like a salad too."

"Go ahead, order two salads, I'm easy."

Garcia had removed a VCR from another box and from the third, a large number of video tapes. A worrisome number.

Garcia seemed to read his mind.

"Relax — you won't have to watch all these tapes. I have them cued. Piece here, piece there. That's video. Images popping."

One thing Vazquez liked about Garcia, he seemed to enjoy his profession. Just unboxing the equipment and hooking it up gave him pleasure and seemed to make him more excited.

As if again reading his mind, Garcia offered, "I know I'm slightly electric. When I walk by the image flutters. And the sound jumps. OK. I'm electric. But that's video. That's film. Movement. Action. Swift. Images. On Parade. I'm electric. So's the business. Bim Bam Boom."

And to the rhythm of his bim bam boom, Garcia had tossed in a cassette, turned on the VCR and the monitor, and hit the volume up button.

"Would you mind lowering..."

Garcia hit the volume down button without looking, the way a typist could hit the bracket keys without looking.

"This is a piece I did for a politician. Guy running for congress." Bim Bam Boom. Cassette stopped. Ejected. New one popped in. Play. "This is a piece I did in Spanish to get Latinos out to vote." Bim Bam Boom. "This is a piece I did which was poetic. It wasn't so good. But look at this image." Bim Bam Boom. "This is a piece I did for advertising. A stock brokerage house. Wanna look solid."

Vazquez suddenly found himself interested in all of them, disturbed that as he got caught up in one, he was watching another. He had seen people do that at home, madly clicking between channels. How could you decide what you were looking at if you only paused for 15 seconds?

"Why is everything so fast? Fifteen seconds, twenty seconds, gone. Wouldn't it be better to hold the picture and let me see it?"

"Not necessarily, Mr. Vazquez. You know what a microsecond is?"

"Mr. Garcia, I have worked on atomic clocks where nanoseconds were considered long measures."

"Oh. Sorry. You see the short images. You take them in. You know about subliminal?"

"I do."

"Then let me come in from a different angle. In video, long is boring; 45 seconds is ages. That's it."

"Mr. Garcia, would you mind if I watched something from beginning to end?"

"Not now. Here comes our salad. By the way you can call me Gary."

John's salad dressing had a distinctive vinegary side that Vazquez enjoyed, but John's never served you a glass of water. You always had to ask.

When the pizza arrived, Mr. Gary Garcia, President of GG Productions, wanted to know what half of the pizza had the "fish." Vazquez guessed that Garcia found even the word "anchovy" repellant. Vazquez ate with gusto asking the waiter for additional oregano, and reminding him that he had asked for water.

"I'm going to show you just under twelve minutes of tape about a minority man who is a specialist in jet engines and their failure. They fly him around the country testing engines and supervising their overhaul and maintenance. He says 'take it out' people take the engine off a plane. Knocking down three hundred thou a year at least. You remind me of him in this; he wanted breakfast. Anywhere he could get grits. And eggs."

Vazquez was trying to be open minded. He didn't like the bim bam boom, the hard slapping of cassettes and buttons. You were supposed to treat tools and equipment with care. He remembered the sergeant in the Air Force who brought a summary court-martial against an airman who had thrown a vacuum tube voltmeter onto a table.

But what he watched seemed well done. A black man who had gone to college at night, studying engineering at City College in New York. In one part somebody asks him why he wears bow ties, and he answered, "because they don't dangle down into an engine when I bend down to look inside." It was funny and a nice touch. The picture looked clean, the music was very nice. And the man had been treated with a lot of dignity. It was a little jarring in places that cut between scenes.

"Not bad," he said out loud to Garcia.

"Not bad? I won awards for this piece." Garcia was obviously hurt, but he kept on talking. "Now I'm gonna do Latinos. Your face all over America. Inspiring kids. And old folks too."

"A clock is not as dramatic as a jet."

"That's what Cordero said about radios. Not drama OK. Human interest. Man with talent. Specializing, in a nation of people who no longer know how to do anything themselves. A nation of men and women who push paper in faceless corporations. Men and women who are not sure what they have to do with what the company does. Then there is you. A man with a specialty. You do one thing from start to finish. With your hands. Know something. No executive bathroom and no desire for one. Eager to go to work in the morning. Unsung fame. Underground stars. That's what plays. Let me show you another. A whole commercial."

The "whole commercial" wasn't sixty seconds long, but it was very effective raising questions of corruption against an incumbent who had been in office a very long time in New York.

"Mr. Garcia I have to get back to work now, but I want to ask you two questions."

"OK Mr. Vazquez, I guess you'll never call me Gary. Shoot."

"Why don't you make one about yourself as a success in the film and video world?"

Garcia pursed his lips, and then said, "Nooooo. I wouldn't even know — naw, I don't like egovid. What's the other question?"

"Did you take photos of me through the store window?"

Garcia got visibly upset. "Mr. Vazquez, I never take pictures of anybody without their permission. I frequently carry a still camera, but I only take pictures of projects I'm working on."

Vazquez started to dig into his pocket for money, and Garcia said, "Forget it. On me. Leave the tip if you want, but I want you to think about this — if the Latino men and women of America who are making it in interesting occupations don't cooperate with me how will the kids know that the world is full of interesting and fulfilling jobs? How? How will the people who are full of prejudices toward Latinos ever get to see us as decent and contributing citizens?

How? Mr. Vazquez, I don't do this for money. I do it to meet my Puerto Rican burden. White man thought he had a burden. I think I got a burden. I can make money in commercials and other projects. But I gotta do this and people like you gotta help me. Otherwise, how do we change the image? How? Think about it Mr. Vazquez. We're making America great, so why are we hiding it? Think about it."

"I will, Mr. Garcia, I will. Goodbye."

"Mr. Vazquez, do I have to tell you that I'm in a rush? Time is everything to me."

"And I have nothing but time. Goodbye."

MONDAY

"Mr. VanBramer? This is Mr. Vazquez. I need to discuss a matter about your clock. Yes. I'm working on it. I have taken it completely apart. I have to have a new arbor and wheel cut for it Mr. VanBramer, or else the clock will never run right."

"Max, you do whatever you have to do to make that clock work and chime. When will you have it ready?"

"Mr. VanBramer, I'm trying to tell you that I have to fabricate a new arbor and wheel. I have to put a new piece into your old clock."

"Do it. When will you have it ready?"

"I don't know yet. When is your election?"

"Oh no you don't Max. I asked first."

"I really don't know yet. If the machinist is busy it might take two weeks to get the new wheel cut. Then six weeks after that."

"Well, don't talk to me anymore, call the machinist now and get busy. Two months is better than seven."

"Mr. VanBramer, I'm talking about having to make a whole new part for the clock. This is an important restoration question."

"Get it."

When VanBramer hung up, Vazquez started laughing and Livrehomme asked him why he was laughing.

"I guess I never learn. Mr. VanBramer doesn't give a damn what I do to his clock. Bottom line for him is to get it before the election. If it only works for two minutes after he is elected he wouldn't care. I thought he would object to making a new part. You know what I think Mr. Livrehomme? I think I could get a quartz movement with a chime, stick it in the case and bring it to VanBramer tomorrow, and he wouldn't even look in the case. He just wants to see it run."

Livrehomme had already reassembled the Seth Thomas and was parsimoniously applying minute quantities of clock oil to the tips of the escape wheel teeth. "We laugh at them, but look at how fast they have gotten us to work on their clocks. Meanwhile I'm embarrassed to take $1500 dollars from this man for this job."

"He forced you. He's crazy."

"Speaking of which, when are you making the video?"

"Mr. Livrehomme, I haven't decided yet. The kid makes good speeches. But I haven't been famous these many years, so what's the rush? By the way, who do you think should play me in the movie?"

Livrehomme laughed and Vazquez laughed.

JOHNNY UNITED

I

Johnny United worked in his stepfather's *bodega* on Lexington Avenue and 109th Street. He had worked Monday through Fridays from as soon as he got out of Galvani Junior High School, which was around 3:15, to nine at night. He worked thirteen hours on Saturdays. Sundays he worked from 8 a.m. to noon. Delivering groceries, unloading trucks and loading basements and stacking cans and moving 100 pound sacks of rice, beans and coffee, had made Johnny United muscular. In High School, Benjamin Franklin High School, he looked older than the other students, older than his sixteen years, because of his size. He worked a little less now from Monday to Fridays, because Franklin was on 116th Street and Pleasant Avenue, and it took much longer to walk back home from school.

Johnny United never complained.

He didn't mind the hard work. He regretted that it was all for his stingy stepfather. Not all. Some was for his mother.

Early Sunday morning was Johnny United's favorite time. Especially in the summer. Although he was working he was already relishing the afternoon game to come. And Sundays was a light day anyway. The work consisted only of working behind the counter, taking care of the occasional customer buying a bottle of milk and a loaf of sliced bread. Nobody bought much on Sundays and nobody delivered anything at all on Sundays. Sometimes families would stop in to get soda to take to the beach, or ask him for things he didn't have, like sand buckets for the kids.

Over on 107th Street there was a convergence of stickball players from some of the near blocks of Spanish Harlem and Italian Harlem. Early in the morning some of the players would be out on the block moving the few parked cars that had been left overnight. Old Dodges and DeSotos, Fords and a few Pontiacs. Usually not more than six cars were in the whole block on a Sunday morning, and usually the ball players knew the owners of at least three.

The car owners were so used to the routine of reparking their cars that they frequently parked on Saturday night around the corner on Lexington in front of the Star Theater, or else they threw their car keys out the window so the players could move the cars.

Johnny United was not too poor to have a bicycle, but he did not have a bicycle, and his stingy stepfather who had a booming business on a well traveled corner just one block from the subway didn't own a car. The few people in the neighborhood who could afford a car took off early on a summer Sunday, packed their families into their four doors, and took off for exotic places like Jones Beach or South Beach early in the morning, some lucky neighborhood kid riding the running board all the way down the block to the corner of Park Avenue, then running back up the block to tell everybody how exciting it had been.

The day didn't always start with stickball. Some of the older Italians liked to play a game called punch ball. The pitcher used the same Spaulding Hi-Bounce as in stickball, and threw it in the same one hop to the plate — the batter stood over the manhole cover and punched the ball with his fist. The best hitter in punch ball was a tall sandy haired Italian called Don who lived in the same block as Johnny United. Everybody liked to watch him bat; he never missed a pitch that he went after. Johnny United never saw him play stickball, but Don often backed the Italian teams in the big money games.

On Friday Johnny United had taken the route back home from school that took him past his old Junior High. Not for sentimental reasons, but because the broom factory was near the school. There he purchased two new broom sticks — he didn't like to take the sticks from old brooms because he believed that the two nails that were used to attach the wire and corn bristles weakened the stick and made it an inferior bat for stickball. He sneaked the broom sticks into the *bodega's* basement and put them next to where he had the tape.

Sunday when he was alone in the store, he meticulously wrapped the lower part of the broom stick in Johnson and Johnson's Red Cross Adhesive Tape. The narrow white tape in a spiral made a bright contrast on the dark blue and dark green bats. And although he worked slowly, like a doctor bandaging a patient, he couldn't wait to get to 107th Street. Johnny United sanded the unpainted last six inches of the stick — the part where the bristles would have been attached. After the sanding, the stick was now a real stickball bat. Next he oiled his glove, and fussed with the leather thongs that kept it together. He had never seen one come loose, or rip, but nevertheless he checked all the knots to be sure they were secure.

He loved Sundays, because there was no stepfather. Just the old toothless man who worked the counter in exchange for food. Johnny United's stepfather didn't believe in paying salaries. He believed in equations though — I did this for you equals you do this for me. Even Johnny United's mother never got any cash. When Johnny United asked his mother why he couldn't get paid — just a little — and why she never had any money either — she just said, "You have everything and I have everything. You have your own room, and no beatings. Give thanks to your stepfather. When you are older you will understand what it means to have everything. Be grateful, he doesn't beat you or me, and doesn't drink. We're never short of food, or short of anything."

Except money. Which you needed to buy tape, broom handles, and which you needed to bet on your games, bet on your own team. Take a girl out for a malted.

II

On 107th Street, the teams were starting to form. Don had chosen his favorite Captain, Chops, who was also a third baseman. And Terry, who always backed the Puerto Rican team, had picked Lefty to be his Captain. Lefty had lost one joint on each of two fingers of his left hand. A policeman had taken a bat away from kids playing stickball and thrown it down the manhole. As soon as the cop was out of sight, the kids picked up the manhole cover and one of them went down into the sewer and brought back the bat. But when they were dropping the heavy iron cover back on the open hole, it slipped from somebody's hand and pinched Lefty's two fingers, severing the first joints. Lefty, who had already recovered from Infantile Paralysis and walked with a limp, taught himself to pitch right handed, just as easily as he had taught himself to ride a bike with a withered left leg. He batted lefty, and it seemed impossible to imagine him as a better hitter. And even with the lame leg he was still faster than a lot of other players.

The captains started picking players, eight to a side, as stickball was played without a catcher. A catcher was unnecessary since there was no calling of balls and strikes — each player had latitude as to how many pitches he could take before swinging. There was no rule as to how many pitches he could let go by, but impatient players waiting their turn at bat, would jeer the batter if he was taking too long. So would spectators, so that jeering was just as effective as counting balls and strikes. And Captains would skip over players who were known to stand up there and wait and wait — it was a sign of a poor player.

Just as in the boxing matches, there were prelims — fights where beginners would dance around, warming up the crowd for the main bout. Even the Golden Gloves followed this routine, with the skinniest kids going first, their stick arms out of proportion to the stuffed glove. And while Johnny United taped, sanded and oiled, the younger stickball players played warm-up games, getting a chance to show their stuff — light betting, $2 a man, but while everything was a prelim, the games were played with a lot of heart, as if each game was a big league World Series game.

Terry was talking to Lefty, while they watched a prelim.

"Is Johnny United going to be here on time?"

"Ain't he always?"

"The big game is gonna cost me $200 if you lose, Lefty. I ain't gonna put no $200 on youse if Johnny United ain't playing."

"So let me go over to the store and talk to him. I'll be back in a flash. Put Jackie in to pinch hit."

"Jackie? That kid can't do nothing right."

"So what? Let 'im play, we're way ahead. Le'me go."

Lefty walked the two blocks quickly to l09th Street and whistled from the sidewalk. None of Johnny United's friends ever entered the *bodega*. It was a message for the stepfather.

"I can't go yet, but I'll be there for sure. I got two new beauties." Johnny United ducked back in the store and showed them to Lefty.

"You gotta come — it's gonna be a $200 game! No lie!"

"25 dollars a man?" asked Johnny United wiping his palms on his trouser legs. That's the highest we ever played for."

"25 a man. Hurry up. I gotta get back."

"Lefty, can you lend me some money?"

"How much?"

"25 or 50."

"Crazy?"

"Come on man, I'll pay you back."

"I ain't got 25 bucks — whatchu need it for?"

"I'm going to run away from home."

"You gonna run away from home with my 25 bucks? Whatchu think, I'm stupid? See ya. Hurry up, we ain't got a lot of time."

III

In the last half of the ninth inning the Puerto Ricans were losing 2-1. There was a man on second and Johnny United came to bat. He took his dark blue beauty and looked at it as if he had never seen it before. He shook it to feel its weight and swung it with one hand. On the very first pitch he ran into the ball with his well known skip step and brought his broomstick square across the center of the Spaulding, and the ball took off on a low trajectory that carried it across Lexington and half way toward Third Avenue. It was a spectacular drive — nobody had ever hit a ball that far before. The outfielders were used to backing up ten to fifteen feet when Johnny United came to bat, but he still put it over their heads.

The man on second easily scored, tying the game and sending the onlookers on the stoops and the ones who stood on the sidewalk's edge into a roar and applause, and Johnny United rounded second going faster than a thoroughbred in the home stretch. And then a child of four or five broke from the crowd and ran into the street between third base and home plate, right in the path of Johnny United coming down as fast and as hard as a human being was able to run.

There was nothing Johnny United could do to avoid the collision. He was both running and looking back over his left shoulder to see where the ball was, trying to gauge whether he had time to get all the way to home plate, or if he should stop at third. When he saw the child in his way, he did the only thing he could think of doing — tried to leap over the child — but it was too late. He kicked the child about mid-body and both went down against the hot tar, "thunk". Even in his falling Johnny United was trying to twist, trying not to fall on top of the child, trying to convert his momentum into a force that would get him to home plate.

Johnny United was tagged out one and one half feet in front of home plate.

Everyone was in an uproar — "He's safe, he's out, we won, you gotta do it over, *afangoul,* why didn't you kill him, pay up the money, fuck you he's gotta do it over, who told him to slow down, *ougotz* you won, we ain't gonna do it over, *ougotz, ougotz,* it's a home run, fuck you, we won 3-2, *afangoul, maricon, maricon, tu madre, strunso!"*

Johnny United was looking at the kid, who had a welt on his rib cage. The father was saying it was the kid's fault and apologizing to Johnny United. Friction burns and tar were all over Johnny United's legs and arms, but he had no major wounds, no broken bones.

In the commotion and yelling of the spectators and the teams, only the gamblers looked cool. The teams were falling into another mood. Only Lefty and Chops yelled at each other now. Chops had a father who was always in a black Cadillac. Louie Bananas, the fantastic outfielder who had made the long throw to home, had found his father shot to death in a parked car on Second Avenue.

The Puerto Ricans had heard of the Black Hand, and all the silent terror that it implied, but the fight now would have to be on the street. Spider, the kid who played second base would have one, maybe two, switch blade knives on him, and Lefty himself would likely have a gun in his gym bag. A real gun, not a homemade or a zip gun.

As the teams sized each other up, a quiet fell, and everyone turned to Don and Terry. The players were keyed to look for the first punch, and then mayhem would start. But Don and Terry were talking quietly.

Terry said, "The game is definitely tied."

Don said, "I don't want no fight on the block."

Terry said, "Me neither. Let me talk to my captain."

When Terry came over, the team crowded around him. Johnny United was crying and saying, "I shoulda creamed that kid, I coulda gone right through him but I didn't have the heart. *Coño,* I didn't do it."

Terry said calmly, "you did right Johnny. You coulda killed that kid. The kid is worth more than the game, worth more than the money. I know money. I know death, believe me. You think about that father. You're a hero Johnny — you hit the longest ball ever — who's gonna take that away from you? You did a good thing — who's gonna take that away from you? Those are dollars you'll never lose. Come on let's figure out what to do."

Danny who was an up and coming good ball player said, "Look Terry, let Johnny go back to third — he made that base safe, so why not? Next batter is Lefty and then me. I know we'll bring Johnny United home. We'll get him in, I mean it Terry."

Privately Terry didn't like that arrangement. The pressure on Lefty and Danny to get a hit would be too much and the odds were they would blow it. Don would go for it because he would calculate the odds the same way, but maybe not. Now the whole game would pivot on one batter, on one strikeout, on one hit — like a winner take all — like a sudden death. Terry liked long shots, but he didn't like this one. He also never wanted to let his team down, his kids down. He never wanted anyone to think he was cheap, either.

"OK," said Terry, "let's offer it."

Don looked down at his loafers. Didn't like it. Figured the odds were for Terry. Fucking Lefty with no fingers and a bum foot, and you still had to be scared of him. And after Lefty was still Danny. Fucking Danny, you never knew what he could do. He was up and coming, the kid was gonna be murder by next year. And Don knew that if he didn't accept, everyone would know he was scared of Lefty. And Danny. Fucking Danny, who last year could barely make a team.

So Don said, "He can go back to third, but you gotta give one out."

"No good, the man made third safe, where do you get off we gotta give an out?"

"That's what we give. Don't forget we tagged him out altogether. Kid or no kid, we tagged him out."

"But the game is tied, right?"

"Right, tied," answered Don.

"Then let's call the greatest game of the year off — nobody loses."

Don looked down the very sharp crease in his slacks to his loafers, each of which had a very shiny penny. He might have been trying to calculate the offer on his toes. Then he looked up and asked, "Terry, how come you always put your money behind the Puerto Ricans?"

"I always go for long shots, Don. And they haven't done bad by me. Your boys never tromped them. They're winners, my kids."

"They don't play bad," conceded Don, "if they played bad we wouldn't want their money. Your money either. Could you tell them Puerto Ricans that they don't scare us, that they don't run the neighborhood yet?"

"Don, I'll bet you that next year will be the last of these games, and in three years there won't be any Italians on this block, and in five years there won't be any Italians in the neighborhood at all. So who's afraid of who? Don, you better look around. Our people are throwing in the chips and getting out of here. Angelo is selling the diner, Little Max is giving up the record store. You know what I'm talking about. Our people are getting the hell out of East Harlem."

"Terry, I tell you what I regret. I regret that kid Johnny United ain't Italian. You sure he ain't got some Italian blood in him?"

"You live in his block — ask his mother," said Terry laughing.

IV

Johnny United said to Lefty, "Today's my day for running."

Lefty said to Johnny United, "We showed them Italians. What a fucking shot you hit. You put it in the second manhole of the next block."

"Lefty, you lend me the 25 bucks, I'll pay you back."

"Hey, I'm talking about the game. You would have been home a half hour before the throw came in — even with that arm Louie Bananas' got."

"I'm talking about 25 bucks."

"Where you going with 25 bucks? I don't think it's enough to run away with. My father pisses me off too. You need more. But here's eight dollars — it's all I got. Whatchu gonna do?"

"I don't know Lefty. First I'm gonna run away. I'm a man. Then I'm gonna do something. Keep your eight bucks. I'll see you next Sunday, but don't tell nobody."

Johnny United opened the store and went to his hiding place. He removed all the money he had saved from tips for delivering groceries. And money he had saved from his winnings, since Terry always gave the team members a couple of bucks when they won. He also went to the place where his stingy stepfather hid his money, and he carefully counted out 25 dollars. And then he ran away from home.

MALIG; MALIG & SAL; SAL.

I

MALIG;

Malig stepped out of the bath wondering why they didn't put showers in the bathrooms of public housing projects. A bath always takes far longer than a shower, even when you hurry. When Sal offered to hook up a shower for them, the housing manager had said it was prohibited. Her dumb mother had asked instead of just doing it. Now they sent a guy around to look at the apartment regularly. Before that, you never saw one of them bastards. Sal was right, you should never tell a landlord nothing.

Standing in front of the mirror still wet, she began to place a few large rollers in her hair and a few small ones. Her mouth full of pins and a cigarette, her hair brush held under her arm, she was leaning close to the mirror, trying hard to keep all the elements under control, straining to see what she was doing. She had promised herself a pair of contact lenses. One of the salesmen at RexCo had told her that she could get a pair and full exam for $230 and that included insurance against loss. She was terribly nearsighted and had to wear thick glasses, but even if they had been thin, she was ready for a drastic change in her life, and that had to include her appearance.

The rollers were in place nice and tight. And she sprayed them with a new "Wet Fixer" she picked up at the drugstore the day before. She was going to cut her hair still shorter, and dye it a different color, and start some exercises to make her breasts a size, and maybe two, bigger. And Sal was right — she had to do something about her round shoulders — other exercises and more concentration on how she stood.

She left the bathroom and went to the kitchen, opened her refrigerator and took out a bottle of Tom Collins mix and a bottle of Maraschino cherries. On the table she had laid out a bowl full of ice cubes, some lemons, an orange, a sharp knife and a candle. She was going to give Sal a party tonight. She plunked two cubes into a glass, poured in the mix, added a cherry and some syrup. Then she walked to her room and pulled the gin bottle from where it was hidden, poured a drink into the mix, stirred it, took a slug and then took out the pint of Bacardi Rum and the bottle of wine from the same hiding place. She never knew what Sal would be drinking, but she had gotten everything he liked including twelve cans of Schaefer beer. He could drink when he felt like it. She brought the bottles back to the kitchen and with her drink in her hand she took a tour of the apartment looking for anything out of place, discovering something slightly erotic in the idea of being very naked, very free.

When she saw the clock in the decorated mirror hanging over the sofa in the living room, she gulped another quantity of her drink and headed back for the bathroom, where she started to put her make-up on. Almost immediately she could see that someone had been in her make-up bag, and her little brush for applying eye liner was gone. Straight for her kid sister's room, she decided, since her mother always was decent enough to put things back. She hated anybody using her make-up because she paid so much for it and here she was stuck with a mother, a grandmother, two kid sisters, and her own daughter to raid her things. She wondered why they didn't put doors on the closets in the public housing projects, or on the openings into the rooms. These damn curtains over everything made her feel stuffed up. More reasons she should leave.

She found her brush and a couple of tubes of old lipsticks which she thought she had lost, and began putting her make-up on again. How would she tell Sal?

Look Sal, I'm 22 and have a daughter almost three, and I am getting old and I ain't getting any prettier and I need to get away from my family, from you and from my lousy job, and I need somebody to take care of me, to give me a house and a car and the life of a housewife, and good weather and a nice place to live without crowded trains and people inspecting your apartment. I'm tired of life with not enough and debts and too many people in one apartment and no privacy about anything, not even a private tube of toothpaste that somebody else won't use and misuse.

But she couldn't put it like that to Sal because he would say, "move in with me." And then he would say something funny like "I won't brush my teeth ever again." And she couldn't tell him she thought his apartment was a terrible dump and she couldn't understand why he wouldn't take his parent's apartment in the Bronx. That was the whole trouble with him. He wanted just the opposite of the things she wanted. He wouldn't take a real job and she knew he could get one. He didn't want the nice apartment in the Bronx — wanted a shitty one on the Lower East Side because it was "closer." Closer to what she didn't know. But she had known him ten years, gone out with him for two and instead of getting better he was getting worse. Always talking about leaving school, about how he didn't like the people there. But he wouldn't leave, and he steadily was changing, he seemed more unsure of himself, more unsure of what he wanted to do. "Don't you want to make money?" she would ask him, and he would say "I don't know. I don't think so." And what was this bullshit about poetry and writing? And he was getting more complicated and he enjoyed everything less. He didn't want to go to parties, he wouldn't dress up. When he was a teenager he had a reputation for being smart. He had folks who worked and they bought everything he wanted as long as he did well in school. He always had good clothes. And after the service he started to change. Same time he started school. It was a pity, that college was messing up the smartest man she knew. Only he wasn't a man, he might be sometime, but he wasn't one now. The man she had been seeing off and on for a year now from RexCo, he was a man, and ready to take care of her — but he also lacked something. He didn't move her — sex appeal — maybe it was just that he wasn't Latin. He was ready to put up an apartment for her, pay her rent and furnish the place too. And he didn't want any entanglements, he was married and he wanted to stay married. She had thought a lot about his offer. He just wanted a place to get away to, and a girl who would treat him right. He didn't want to know what she did all the time, she just had to reserve some time for him. And he wasn't bad looking, nor stiff like some of the other men at RexCo, and he would take her on a trip now and then. And she was very tempted. She had ideas about letting him keep her and then having Sal around all the time. Nobody moved her like Sal, that was a fact. And she knew that Sal loved her, truly loved her, or else he wouldn't, couldn't, put up with all the shit she gave him. But she was afraid of Sal too. She could play with him, but he wasn't a punk. The guy at the office would accept Sal, but it wouldn't work the other way around. There was a story that Sal had shot a gang kid once in a playground at point blank, and that he had a very violent side, that luckily didn't come out very often. But being kept was only part of an answer, for Howard wasn't rich enough to keep her all the way. She would have to work and there was Linda, her baby. How would she fit in to being kept by Howard and living with Sal part time? It was too crazy but the offer of the apartment had been tempting and she had begun to see in it a real solution. She had to simplify the formula. Find a man who would keep her well, full time. Reduce the men to one instead of two. She couldn't give up Sal for Howard. It was not right. Howard was not enough and Sal was true. So she had decided to leave them both, go to Puerto Rico and start again. Change her looks and her way of life. That would hurt Sal, but it was fair. It was fair for what he had given her that was good.

And that was one of the painful parts. Sal had given her good, very good things and feelings. He was a man in so many ways that she had come to be very fascinated with him. He knew how to move her and that was special. And he had a way of holding her, possessive and proud. But when they went to parties or in public like at the club, he let her have her freedom to come and go and dance with whomever she wanted. And he was jealous, he admitted it, but he said he had to stay in control of things like that, "Or I'll have to kill every man that looks at you, every creep who ogles that behind of yours." And he was generous with his praise and made her feel sexy and attractive and wanted. He didn't do those little things like try to flirt with other girls or act disinterested in her while she was around other men or women. And he had been good to Linda, giving her his time and showing in the way he was with her, the way he talked to that little girl, that he could be a real father, better than her flesh and blood father.

"Sal," she said out loud to the mirror, "I love you but we can't make it." She washed off her right eye and began again. If only he had stayed the way he was when he came out of the service. He had a beautiful little sports car and he dressed in the latest things. Late at night he would take her through the drive in the park going at incredible speeds and doing things with his shift, downshifting he called it, so she thought the car would explode. And when they got to that part of Central Park that was called Snake Hill, she had to close her eyes sometimes the way he would go down that hill the car swaying from side to side and going round on two wheels. Yes he was wild, he couldn't stop driving hard, couldn't stay home one night, not one night in the week, and if he went to a movie then he'd find another place to go afterwards, and it was out 'til one or two in the morning every night. And two or three times a week he borrowed his father's red and white Oldsmobile and they would wind up in the back seat and he would ball her. Sometimes in his father's garage, sometimes in Central Park. They would leave the car and go off into the bushes. The first time they ever balled was in the park. He had said, "Goddamn it Malig, if you blow in my ear again, I'm gonna ball you right here." It had been a crazy scene that night since she was wearing skin tight slacks. And they were afraid together, and afraid of being in the park, and of being seen. And she blew in his ear again. So they took her slacks off only one leg and her panties the same, and they made love in a most uncomfortable position but it had been good good. Once they had been caught making love in the park. Sal had stopped in one of the parking areas, and next thing they knew they were balling right in the front seat. The windows of the car were all steamed up and a cop knocked on one of them. Sal, without getting up, rolled down the window and said, "Yes Sir?" The cop said, "I'm going to be back in fifteen minutes. You better not be here." Sal didn't like that, didn't like the police, and after that he never stopped in the park again. "Too many stories of cops raping girls who are afraid to talk because they have to explain too much. I'm not putting you in that spot again." After that he had started sneaking her in and out of his mother's apartment and finally he had gotten a sort of begrudged permission to have Malig over as a "guest" now and then. It meant that they could sleep late.

Then he sold the sports car. Then he said he was not going to the movies anymore. Then he quit a really good job he had. Then one night he walked into her apartment and pulled the cord out of the T.V. Yanked it right out. While the set was on. What a fight they had that night. That's when her family decided he was crazy. After that her grandmother called him *El Loco*. *"Como esta El Loco, Malig?"* And then she would roar with laughter as if she could see the scene of Sal pulling the cord out of the T.V. The live wire sparking in his hands. Then he moved out of his mother's house, took a nice apartment in Brooklyn. Big rooms and he left in three months. Moved to the Lower East Side to the awful apartment he had now. A bathtub in the kitchen. Even the projects didn't have bathtubs in the kitchen. And then he disappeared for a whole week. Nobody knew where he was and when he reappeared he said he had been drunk — drunk for five days or seven days or eight days maybe. And when he was asked why he had done that, he said he "didn't know." And he read more and more and said he was doing worse and worse in school, and he started writing. Carrying papers with him and scratching at them all the time, but that gave him no peace either. He had no peace and she didn't know why. And when his mother and father decided to go to Puerto Rico and offered him their very nice apartment in the Bronx and he said no, that was the beginning of the break. That same week she took up Howard's offer of a drink. And she felt that Sal had driven her away.

Exactly.

That's just what she would tell him. She looked at her eyes now. They seemed right. And she started working on her face with a powder brush.

"Sal," she was gonna say, "you drove me away. Not that you stopped loving me or you weren't nice to Linda, or that you found other women, or started flirting, or became careless or cruel. You started driving me away with your behavior — looking sloppy all the time. And the things you said like you weren't going to finish college, or that you didn't wanna work. Those things drove me away. And when you started writing I liked that. I thought it would be good for you because writers don't work like other people work, but they use their brains and they make good money. But you don't write anything. Anything you write you cross out or throw away, or say you have to write it again. A writer has to write.

How can I believe you will be a writer if you haven't written anything in more than a year?"

Malig ran to the living room to check the time. She had time for another drink and made herself one. Then she stood in the door of the living room staring at the clock set in the mirror. On the ends of the mirror were two pink flamingoes and around the top edge of the mirror, over the clock, there was a bouquet of many flowers in green and gold. God, it was ugly. Sal was always saying that it was so ugly it was actually beautiful, and that the world was going to begin when the two terrible flamingoes came alive.

When he talked like that it bothered her. Because he could be so serious about it and use all his Sunday words to say that the world had not yet actually begun. That we were all here on earth as a trial. That there would be so many generations and no more. When that time came the clock would decide if man had done well enough to let the world begin. If the discoveries of science and the contributions of art were greater than the evils of war and poverty and exploitation and the misery of people who had to live in rotten conditions, then the world would begin. He hoped now wasn't the time, Sal said, because if now was the time the world would not begin. The clock was God, the flamingoes were angels, and the mirror was the whole universe including heaven because you could see everything in it.

When he talked like that it displeased her because she wasn't sure whether he was serious or not. He sounded serious but she had the feeling that he was making fun of something, himself, her religion, everything. Had college made him crazy? Her mother used to say that too much studying, too much reading, could make people go crazy. It was bad for the *cerebro*. A well known fact in Puerto Rico. Especially if the person doing the reading and studying does not eat nourishing foods like eggs, avocados, breadfruit and fresh coconuts, water and flesh. That's what Sal's father told her once. And here was Sal eating nothing, drinking too much, not sleeping well, just reading and going to school and doing odd jobs. Maybe he had gone crazy. Maybe all he needed was vitamins. What was it he had said had made him get drunk for a week? He said he had read three books in one week that had depressed him. What were their names? If for no other reason, she should remember them just to be sure not to read them. And who was forcing him to live in rotten conditions? And it was not nice to fool around with God, to say that God was a clock. She had met a girl who had gone out with Sal when he was fifteen, and the girl had said, "Sal's too smart for himself. Smart people are unhappy. Get yourself a nice dumb guy. Sal's been too spoiled by his family, too spoiled by his brains. He don't know what work is, what wanting something is. He never had to do it."

She began to dress, put her eyeglasses on, was satisfied with the thin black lines she had drawn and the faint blue shadow on the upper lids. How well her eyes would look when she would be rid of her glasses. She began to pull the rollers out carefully from her hair and to brush as carefully. She had put on her white dress, the one Sal said drove him wild. No stockings over her beautifully tanned legs. And no panties tonight either. The dress fit beautifully and even the sheerest panties made lines. Tonight she wanted Sal to jump right out of his skin. For she was going to give him a good, very good, good-bye. She wanted him to remember her. Even if she didn't read the books he gave her, and if she hadn't taken the courses or gotten interested in anything that he recommended. They had had sex between them in a beautiful way. She wanted to be remembered by him powerfully, perhaps, because she was afraid that that was how she would remember him. She had difficulty remembering herself in bed with her husband. Tried to remember her dismal marriage, her dismal furnished room with a toilet in the hall. God, everyone in one room, sleep, eat, watch TV, cook. After a while she was grateful that the toilet was outside. It was a break from the monotony of that little cell and it was a chance to be alone although not for long, not with four other families sharing two toilets. She could not remember sex with her husband, although it wasn't that long ago, just that it wasn't pleasant. More like washing dishes, that kind of thing you have to do which ain't really terrible but you don't ever enjoy it. And Howard was boring. And anyway he was so white he looked like a boiled fish and so she was put off. Poor Howard. In a way he took more shit than Sal. Howard spent money on her — restaurants, perfumes, clothing here and there, a very nice watch last Christmas, and what did he get for it? A very moody girl who had gone to bed with him three times in one year, once because she was curious to see the hotel he offered. But she was not going to waste her sympathy on Howard. Howard was a big wheel at RexCo, he was knocking down big bucks and had his wife and house in the country somewhere. His wife could go to the beauty parlor twice a week. She had her own car. What the shit more could she want? And Howard had the story straight from the beginning. Malig had told him he would get nowhere. He persisted in spending his money on her. If he thought what he spent was worth three cold bangs in one year that was his business. After each rotten time with sex, Malig had told Howard she was sorry. She had apologized and told him it would not be any better ever. She had tried to spare his feelings. In fact hadn't she gone to bed with him in the first place because she cared about his feelings? What the hell — it was true he was a *gringo,* but that did not mean she could be cruel to him. No, there was absolutely no point in being sorry for Howard. She had been straight, very straight, with him. But not with Sal. Imagine if Sal ever found out about Howard! Holy shit. There would be hell to pay. It was a frightening thought because Sal was capable of killing her for something like that. He tried to fight his jealousy and she knew it, and she took advantage of the fact, often manipulating him into something simply by asking him if he was jealous. But being unfaithful, and with a *gringo*! And with a *gringo* that she didn't even love or respect. How would she say to him "Look I just felt sorry for the man, so I went to bed with him. There was no feeling, I wasn't even disgusted." How could she expect Sal to understand such a thing. Sal who was so straight, so honest, so child-like when it came to these things.

No.

The best idea was had. She had to say goodbye to Sal. Goodbye to Howard. Howard would be easy. One phone call. Sal would require a night, perhaps two nights, passionate love making and careful, very careful explanations. He would respect anything that was well thought out. She would have to lie and say she already had a job in Puerto Rico. Sal would never accept a scheme which did not include a job. If she presented the plan in terms of personal goals of her own fulfillment, her own freedom, he would accept it. Because he genuinely only wanted the best for her. He had told her once, "If I thought I was bad for you, or that I was keeping you back, I would get out of your life." And it wasn't just a line. Sal had a way of saying and meaning things like that. He said them very simply and very directly, and those were the things he meant. He had also said, "If I thought you were fucking around on me I would take it very badly and I don't know what I would do." And that was true. Sal didn't like to make threats and he also disliked violence. "Only people who can't think use violence. Violence is for stupid people. Smart people never need it, they know better ways of achieving the things they want."

Perhaps she was making a big undue fuss over this parting. She could do it more easily through one or two small lies. She could start by saying that her grandmother's sister was dying and that she had to go to Puerto Rico. Then once she was in Puerto Rico, she could write and say she had been offered a nice job. Then she could write and say she took it. Sal was too wild to sit around waiting for her, too smart not to figure out what was happening after a short time. This way it would seem more natural, his feelings would be spared. She could say she met a nice man. He was proposing marriage. She intended to accept. She would never forget Sal, but she knew he would understand.

No.

She looked at herself in the mirror. A white dressed devil. She took a short gulp from her drink. Said, "Sal, the world is about to begin for me. I cannot do it by small lies."

And then she took a long gulp from her drink.

II

MALIG & SAL;

Malig put the light on by pulling the string dangling from the ceiling in the middle of the room, for the New York City Housing Authority in its economic wisdom put in string pulls instead of wall switches for all the lights. Whenever she complained about the string pulls Sal would say it was prejudice. "Since they're only building these things for blacks and Puerto Ricans they make sure they remind you of your place. Malig, it's prejudice

— if they were fair they would put in doors, showers and balconies too."

When she opened the door, the first thing Sal saw was the mirror with the clock and flamingoes, but he was not struck with the mixed feeling of hideousness and hilarity that it usually evoked, because what he saw this time was his own strange face. Strange because of how it flashed upon his eyes and mind; as if it were the sallow portrait of another person painted by an indifferent artist. Was the face so expressionless because the artist was indifferent or was it because the interplay of conflicting thoughts and emotions worked to create a nothing upon his face?

"You really hate those flamingoes, don't you?"

"I wasn't looking at them this time. I was thinking that it made a nice surreal portrait. My expressionless face with a clock over my head and a flamingo on each shoulder. The only passion in the composition the incredible red color of the birds."

"What would you like to drink?"

"Anything. I had a drink with Carlos — the junky, my friend."

"Come into the kitchen, so I don't have to yell," yelled Malig.

Sal stepped into the kitchen and looked at it as if for the first time.

"Malig, let me see your face. You have a nice face. I don't have any face at all. Abraham Lincoln is supposed to have said that when a man was thirty-five or forty he was responsible for his face."

"Yeah, but you're not thirty-five or forty. Ouch. I almost cut my finger."

"You know what? This kitchen has a sad brown Puerto Rican face. When you see a picture of an American kitchen all the appliances have happy faces and expressions on them. They look content and they look wise. And appliances are blond with beautiful blue eyes just like all the Americans."

Malig thought of Howard's blue eyes as she passed Sal a Bacardi and Coke with a big chunk of lime.

"Maybe I got it backwards," continued Sal taking a long appreciative pull from his drink with its real fresh lime instead of a squirt of Realemon which was what they gave you at the club. Or the sweet Sneaky Pete wine Carlos liked to drink.

"The problem is the other way around. Americans have no expressions, no emotions, they are like the porcelain enamel, passive — you know, I don't think they ever have orgasms..."

You're right, thought Malig, tight and small and worrisome and painful, and bug me.

"I should have asked Carlos about his sex life with the Park Avenue girl — if he had one — Shorty told me that he had laid in the hospital at Lexington Kentucky for one year unable to get an erection. This is a good drink Malig, what are we celebrating, limes and all?"

"Nothing special."

Malig felt she just couldn't jump into it without some preliminary niceties. Sal was strange tonight. Not because of what he said or how he said it — he always talked on and on about all kinds of stuff comprehensible only to him, and sometimes she wondered if it was even comprehensible to him. It was never sense what he spoke, and he didn't care. "What do I care about sense? Sense is the one thing that don't make any sense to me," he would say and start laughing. He had his manner of speaking about him, but otherwise he was different. He had not kissed her when he came in. He had not touched her, patted her ass, had not tried to goose her or feel her up. He had not tried to coax her out to the stairwell. Yesterday he became strange when they ran into an old schoolmate of his, Guillermo. Guillermo told her that Sal had been the smartest kid in school. When she asked him later if that was true, he was silent for about a block, and then he said, "McKenzie, a black kid was the smartest, but maybe Efrain was, and he is dead, so so so fucking smart dead. So what. Dead and smart is maybe the same thing." And she hadn't said anything after that, falling into a reverie of how she would break the news of her departure. Just put it into positives, of her entry into a new life.

Sal was somebody she could not easily forget but it was clear that they could not be together, could not — could not function. She could not clean house for him or have children or lead a life because he was too much, too strong, too opinionated, too, too, too crazy, crazy, that was the word she always wound up with. He was crazy. How else could you explain his behavior and him? He hated everything — he hated nothing. He said something in the morning and he contradicted himself at night. People with brains were all a little crazy, there was no way around it. They never had any peace. They couldn't do anything without thinking and thinking about everything, like every tiny thing you did, your life depended upon. Shit. Why not do something sometime, and think about it later, or even better still, do it and never think about it? Was it possible that too much reading and bad diet could really make a person go nuts? Weaken the brain, make the *cerebro debil,* as her mother would say? Make him eat avocados and coconuts and fish, and olive oil and you might wind up making him smarter, more analytical more critical. Fuck it. Give him more hero sandwiches — it was all he seemed to want to eat, and let him go on with his clever bullshit entertaining himself as long as he wanted. She was going to Puerto Rico to live — to be free, do whatever came along, shop or steal, to hell with Sal, to hell with her mother, to hell with everybody.

The sudden wave of anger brought a flush to her face, and she blurted it out, "I'm going to Puerto Rico. That's what we're celebrating."

"Give me another drink," said Sal, "when?"

"I got a job," said Malig, "shit I got it again."

"Got what again — a job?"

"My fingernail twice now. Gonna have to cut it off."

"When Malig?"

"I'm waiting for a letter confirming the job and then they're sending me a ticket."

There was a long silence. Sal drank and Malig drank. They sat opposite each other at the narrow ends of the kitchen table. Its tin painted top chipped here and there at the edges. Cigarette burns around the edge. A wooden board, wet with lime juice, a knife, bottles, between them. Sal was not going to talk no matter what. He was trying hard to pitch his ears forward. The black guy at the Post Office who was a weight lifter — body builder, had told Sal that it was possible for a person to flex any muscle of his body — it only required concentration. And the zen people and the yoga people could do more — they could control even the involuntary muscles, slowing their own heartbeat, going into suspended animation. Was that from the Way of Zen or some bullshit from a comic book like *Wonder Woman* or a radio show like *The Shadow,* or was it *Mandrake?* Probably *The Shadow,* who could cloud men's minds and suspend their eyesight. So I will pitch my ear right out over my eyeglasses if necessary because I am not going to give Malig the satisfaction of answering her or commenting, or anything. Her humiliations of me are dead. I will not speak to her ever a-fucking-gain even if the price I pay is a ruptured spleen, or a busted gut from the effort it will take to keep my stupid mouth shut. I shall become a single hand clapping in this brick wilderness eighteen stories high over Harlem, no piece of ass, no swinging hip no beautiful legs no sweet sweet sweet pussy's, fucking worth it.

Malig thought it had gone well. No bullshit. I'm going *punto.* And he hadn't reacted at all. Like maybe he thought she wasn't for real. She had done it well by accident, by not pressing the soonness of it —

like that. She would just take off, send him a postcard. She could say goodbye without actually having to say it — tonight would be the last night, who needed speeches — let him make all the speeches, the less I say the better it will be.

Malig had not noticed Sal tightening up. She was so relieved, so relaxed now that she was beginning to think about having a nice week-end with him. So she said aloud, "It isn't sure yet. One of the salesmen made the contact for me, somebody asked him if he knew a bilingual secretary and he said me."

Sal tried to use a level tone — but he felt the anger rising, the anger gripping his throat, the anger making his heart beat faster — said, "I don't give a fuck Malig. We're finished you and me. I ain't taking two cents worth of your ever fucking lasting bullshit anymore." But the control went after the first word and by the end of the sentence he was on his feet yelling at the top of his lungs, "Go to Puerto Rico and become a prostitute taking four bits from any *Yanqui* who hires you for the ten minute fucks they enjoy, you fucking whore, cause I don't give a fuck."

"Don't call me a whore you faggot!"

"Not only are you a whore, your mother's ..."

Malig took the knife from the table and went to his stomach. Sal jumped, took a cut low on his right arm and grabbed the knife from Malig. He spun and pushed her, sent her flying into the living room where she knocked over a table and lamp, and fell on the floor.

"I don't care if you kill me you faggot. Go back to them faggoty friends of yours in college with your

faggoty books and your faggoty bullshit and your
faggoty words and faggoty ideas. You ain't even a
writer — that junky Carlos has more interesting
stories — you ain't nothing but a baby. You don't
know shit, can't do shit, you ain't Puerto Rican ain't
American, you don't know what you are — but I'll tell
you — you are nothing, a big fucking faggoty na, na,
na."

She came at Sal with the lamp.

III

SAL.

Sal kicked her, pushed her and went after her with
the knife — stiffened his hand and his arm, went to
find her heart, her fucking no good heart if she had
one. He was going to cut it out and eat it. Suddenly he
saw his face in the mirror, blood smeared across it, a
madman — scared him — the mad face with its band
of red, he took his fist and punched the mirror again
and again and again, knife still in his hand, cuts
all over his knuckles, destroyed the red birds,
pounded the face of the clock, traded his red with their
red, smashed smashed smashed, stepped back
breathing so hard it cut his throat, trembling,
couldn't produce his voice, kicking her again and
again, kicking her, ran to the door, out the hall ran to
the stairs smashed the door open fell down the first
flight, stumbled, fell, tripped, flew down the next and
the next and the next and the next and the next, voices

in the yellowed cinder blocks of the stairwell echoing "What is it?" *"Que pasa,"* "Are you alright?" and doors slamming steel doors against steel jambs, and tripping, saliva and sweat in his mouth, and into the lobby then the street, the night, running with the knife in his hand, his mind a hurricane howling "kill her, kill her," a siren, a very loud siren, police are chasing me, run into a one way block against the traffic, run faster, I can't make it don't have the breath, can't breathe my own saliva is so thick it is choking me, my sweat is blinding me, a voice yelling "Hey, hey you crazy fuck in here in here." Carlos. Carlos waving him into a hall, Carlos taking the knife, "Come on you zombie, come on shag ass," running through a hall again a hall out a back door down wooden steps stink of garbage of rags putrefying, a long dark corridor, Carlos ahead, incredible stench of piss, "I'm gonna pass out Carlos I can't run no more," "Give your ass to the cops you shit, don't talk hurry run, come on," up more stairs, then Carlos again, "Jump, jump to the fire escape jump you fucking zombie, don't stand there," a jump a fire escape up up up up voices "Who that out there?" clambering, lost step came down across shin great pain, run up run up, a roof, feet in tar soft under that wants to hold, run over a low wall, across another roof another fire escape, down down, Carlos — "In here, in here, stupid, in here, back up back up into a window," collapsing on the floor one heart beating from shoulder to shoulder no air no saliva, Carlos — "Shut up shut up they'll hear you a mile away," cannot answer, cannot stop gasping, aches, great pain in the leg, Carlos rubbing his back, bringing a wet rag over his face his head, in his mouth sucking water, choking, rolling over flat on the floor, could not breathe on the floor, stood up, toilet toilet, Carlos leading him to kitchen sink, "Piss here," chest still heaving pissed, hot piss which hurt, sudden vomiting, vomiting. Back in the room, "Here's wine, take a taste." Running water, pain in the arm, Carlos — "Who did you stab? Did you kill your girl?" Sal, "No, no," chest heaving, wine tasting like puke in his mouth, dry heaves in his stomach, his throat sore. Carlos — "I wiped the knife and threw it down a chimney stack, even I don't know which one." Sal, "I should have wasted the motherfucker." Carlos, "No, want a smoke?" Sal, "No, I should have killed her." Carlos, "No shut up drink wine. Did you stab her?" Sal, "No." Carlos, "She cut you like that? Your arm your hand, your hand is a fucking mess." Sal, "I smashed God and the terrible angels, punched the shit out of Him, stomped them on the floor, I'm sick man, my fucking leg is killing me." Carlos with wet rag, "Let me see, Jesus, you scraped shin terrible but your hand really looks a mess, stick it in the sink." Sal, "I don't give a fuck, agh, agh, shit." Carlos, "Piece of glass there." Sal, "Hospital." Carlos, "You crazy, walk into a hospital like this you get arrested first, treated second. We take care of it here, put some water to boil." Sal, "How do you turn this on?" Carlos, "Just plug it in." Sal, "Look at this fucking hand," open white flesh trembling, hot blood flowing anew over congealed brown streaks. Carlos, "This fucking water will never boil, these fucking hot plates ain't shit. It ain't gonna stop bleeding 'til I take the glass out." Sal, "You got any aspirin? I can't take this pain in my leg." Carlos, "Don't use that kind of drug," ha ha, "Want a little taste of heroin?" Sal "No." Carlos, "I'll get you some aspirin and bandages tomorrow, drink more wine and suffer, be glad you ain't in jail or shot on the street. Running down the street with a fucking bloody knife — what? You think you're in — a fucking movie? Here. Give me your hand." Sal, "You clean that knife?" Carlos, "What do you think I boiled water for?" Sal, "Agh, agh." Carlos, "Sorry, but here it come, yeah. Here let me clean it with this. Put your arm up now, that hand is gonna be something, must have eight different cuts over it." Sal, "The pain in my leg is a motherfucker." Carlos, "Why don't you lie down? Keep your arm in the air. Drink some more wine." Sal, "My whole body hurts you know, everything." Carlos, "You'll sleep until tomorrow, you'll be sore all over. I'll get you aspirin, can't go in the street tonight. After a few days, you look at your hand a lot, if it is getting green or yellow go to a private doctor, otherwise forget it — you got one cut maybe needs a stitch but if it stops bleeding soon it will be a good sign. Tomorrow I'll put it together with tape so you won't need sewing — I know how to do a butterfly with tape — you think you have any broken bones in there?"

"No. Maybe my leg is broken."

"Na. Your leg ain't broken, it's just that you scraped your shin from here to 114th Street and that is painful but if you got a crack in the bone where you hit the fire escape step, you just stay off the leg for a week and it'll heal itself."

"How will I know I got a crack?"

"It'll hurt you a lot for a few days with a dull pain right here, see. This is where you hit and then scraped up. You had a night huh? You know when you are tired like this pain hurts you more — also you are drunk and tomorrow you got a hangover to deal with."

"I don't give a fuck."

"You think you should have killed her?"

"I should kill my fucking self."

"Bullshit. She's a beautiful girl."

"Jive fucking spic more interested in dancing and makeup and nice clothes. She'll go with anybody who can give her a hundred bucks a week."

"So will any broad."

"She thinks she can go to Puerto Rico and because she's beautiful and bilingual — and she ain't all that bilingual — she's gonna get a great job and catch a millionaire."

"So what, it's 1960, the start of a new decade man, got a hundred young Puerto Rican girls a week going to Puerto Rico from all over New York with the same idea. Ha ha ha. Got a hundred young Puerto Rican girls a week coming to New York with the same idea. Ha ha ha. The new decade they gonna be new people. Can't stop the young women no more. This is modern times. They become nothings — nothings, maybe whores, washed out, bar maids sleeping with lonely men, at thirty they gonna look like fifty, but you can't tell them that. And the ones who come here the same shit. If they become something — what is something? A fucking housewife in the Bronx? An office girl downtown? Is that something? All us Puerto Ricans was born to work for somebody, make babies and drink beer. I'd rather be a junky than be that, a fucking office flunky. They want glamour and money, gonna get routine and browbeating, but they don't know it."

Sal couldn't keep his eyes open anymore. Exhaustion was coming over him like a fresh sheet. In his eyes he saw Little Charlie that night in February in the hallway on 109th Street, eight boys all drinking cheap wine getting ready to go to a party, the hall stinking of cigarettes and wine, and Little Charlie saying to PeeWee, "I love her you know, I mean I love her, and now she won't even dance with me, not even do a fucking mambo with me, man. I know I done wrong, but I don't deserve this, how can I get her back when she won't even do a mambo with me? When they used to play *Babarabatiri* we would take the floor and everybody used to say it man, we were the best, we danced beautiful together, in the Palladium they would make a ring around us, I don't deserve this shit man." And he saw Little Charlie start punching the small window panes in the inner door of the building's entrance. And he punched harder and harder and each time his fist went deeper and deeper through the glass and on the seventh pane he gashed his arm near the elbow, cut his artery and Sal saw himself putting a tourniquet on Little Charlie's arm with his handkerchief, and they took Little Charlie to

Flower Fifth Avenue Hospital, where he got a lot of stitches and had forever after a slightly stiff arm, which showed when he played stoop ball. And Charlie got his girl back.

"Are you asleep?" asked Carlos.

Sal did not answer.

ONE SUNDAY MORNING

I

He knocked at the door marked 3A. A voice inside the apartment said, "Who?" and a dog barked and a cat meowed and a canary tweeted. "Me. Newspaper boy," he responded, adding "Sunday Daily News."

The woman, short and round, with a very beautiful face and long black eyelashes and long black hair, repeated, "Sunday News? You have all the sections?"

"*Si,*" he said, "all of them."

"Including the radio programs?"

"Yes, for the whole week."

"Then come in."

This was the game they played every Sunday morning. He, Sonny, pretended he was a newsboy. His godmother, Titi, pretended not to know who was knocking.

He handed the newspaper to his godmother and said *Bendición,* got his kiss and benediction, and entered the long narrow corridor that went past the bathroom and opened into the living room. Beauty, the blondish little dog, wagged her tail and it banged along the wall of the corridor. Her tiny claws slipped on the linoleum and she fell, fell, and fell. When Beauty wagged her tail, she used her whole body, and she seemed hinged in her middle. Feeri, the Angora cat came out. He was nearly as tall as Beauty, and his great silky fur made him look nearly as round. Feeri came not to greet Sonny, but to be admired and stroked.

"Sonny, what are all the programs on WEAF this week?"

He knew them all, every program and at what time. All of his godmother's favorites not only on WEAF, but on the other stations as well. WJZ, too. On Sunday they had to listen to the Hartz Mountain Canary Hour.

II

His Godmother also had fish.

Fish in three tanks.

One kind called guppies; little tiny tiny fish. Some called Angelfish, others whose names he did not know, that had brilliant stripes along the thumbnail length of their bodies.

She loved animals.

She loved children.

She was godmother to many, many children. She had no children of her own.

They put the radio on. The Canary Hour began with many happy canaries singing, and the announcer would soon talk about why Hartz Mountain made the best canary feed in the United States. The other man, the host, conducted the canaries in their performances. Sonny would listen and let his eyes drift around the room.

Along the top of the wall about 12 inches from the ceiling there was wood moulding. The walls below were painted by a process called "Mickey Mousing." He had seen his father doing it many times. Paint the wall one color, let it dry, then dip a rag in another color and roll it over the first color. But his father never let him try it, never let him paint at all.

On the walls there were framed pictures of hunting dogs. There was a wooden cut-out elephant dancing on one leg. There was a framed black paper silhouette of a face, neck, and shoulders, with a real cloth dress. And as his eye drifted to the bedroom, beyond the open double doors, he saw the bedspread and the fish tanks next to the street windows.

The canaries sang; sometimes in chorus, sometimes in solos, sometimes in accompaniment with recorded music, sometimes without music at all. Sometimes somebody whistled to get the birds started, sometimes the somebody seemed to whistle the whole time. And while their cheerful voices filled the little apartment he stared at the bedspread.

He knew how it was made. The women saved every piece of cloth. His godmother was a blouse and skirt seamstress. His mother was a dress seamstress. Their best friend Carmen Nuñez did not work but also sewed at home. They all had Singer machines at home, "factory models" they called them, and made most of their own clothing and a lot for the children. They bought Simplicity Patterns at the Woolworth's, and cloth at *La Marqueta*. And there were always odd pieces of cloth in a bin or box under or around the sewing machine. When enough of these odd pieces had accumulated, the women would sit in a circle and turn the cloth into little circles or hexagons. Each finished piece was only about 3 inches in diameter. Then they had to be sewn together, and the women decided what went well where. It was time consuming. By hand. No *whirr* and *whoom* of the machine motor starting, winding, and stopping. They called it "yo-yo" for reasons he did not know. Then the whole thing had to be lined. Each woman made one for herself, sharing advice and trading pieces of cloth.

His father forbid him to sew.

His Godmother said to him from the rocking chair, "Sonny it's time to feed the fish and Carlos." The Canary Hour was over.

"Titi, is it true that nightingales sing better than canaries? Papi says that God taught nightingales to sing, but canaries only learned from Angels."

"Your father and his ideas. It's the only time he talks about God or Angels."

She would trail off then, change the conversation, never talk about his father.

The fish were by the front windows so that the sun would warm the water and "give them vitamins." He dusted some fish food from the box. For the canary, Carlos, he had to remove the white cups and take them to the kitchen table. There on an open shelf covered with oil cloth, he would find the Hartz Mountain Canary Food — the bright orange can, with its very yellow canary on the front. He would fill one porcelain cup with bird seed, and the other with water. And he would change the paper lining on the cage bottom.

III

His Titi also liked plants.

Titi also liked porcelain statues, and bisque figures, cut glass dishes and vases, chrome and glass martini shaker sets with matching glasses, blue-glass coffee tables, black iron and red marble smoking stands with ashtrays, carnival glass from the five and dime, ceramic candy and fruit dishes. He did not know what a martini was — neither did his Titi. But she had won the set at the movie house. And she had also gotten a whole set of china, one piece at a time at the local movie house, the Regun Theater on 116th Street.

"Junk." His father would say, "Your godmother likes to collect junk. Including godchildren," while he prepared cornmeal with milk, and sliced apples and raw pumpkin for his nightingale, Keero. "Any piece of junk I find I bring to your mother for your godmother, and she always takes it."

IV

Beauty was always pregnant. Feeri was always siring cats. Carlos found himself sharing the cage one day with a female canary named Libertad, and soon there were eggs in the nest and soon there was Chucho, Jacinto and Jose, in their own cage.

And the plants multiplied as if they were rooted in the Puerto Rican soil with the Puerto Rican sun shining on them. And every available tin can had a plant in it from the Export Soda cracker can to the Danish butter tins. And the fish were multiplying also, and the prune juice bottles, which looked like round cookie jars, had fish in them, and now there were six tanks, even though the mother fish ate most of the babies. Titi had become an expert at predicting delivery and with a little fish net she scooped the newborn fish away from the mother's murderous tiny jaws. Soon one tank was only for pregnant fish, and one was the "nursery," where only babies swam.

Titi was playing her guitar in the rocking chair, when Sonny asked her, "Why didn't you get married and have children?"

She stopped playing and started rocking.

"I got married. I married a very handsome boy named Billy. He was blond and strong and a hard working boy. He was seventeen, and I was only thirteen. But at thirteen I was a woman already, and I wasn't so fat, Sonny, I was slim and very beautiful. He played the guitar and I sang. He was teaching me to play and I was teaching him to sing. He loved music and he loved dancing. We were married about seven months when we went to a dance in Naranjito where your father is from — a little town in the mountains. We went dancing every weekend, and Billy had a Ford that we used to call *'de patitas,'* of little feet. I don't know why it was called like that. In the dance we got separated. I heard noises, there was a fight, there was gunfire, six or seven shots. When the room cleared Billy was laying on the floor dead. So was another man. They had nothing to do with the fight. But they were dead. I was a widow at thirteen. I was pregnant but I had a miscarriage. I lost my baby — do you know what it means?"

"Yes," he answered, not understanding.

"Here, let me show you a picture."

She got up and showed him a picture of a hospital room with her in the bed. There was a strangely tropical light coming in one window onto a white and black checkered floor. Whether time, or the photographer had introduced a slight sepia quality to the photo, Titi did not know. "I think they always came out slightly brown," she said sadly, smelling the photograph. "It's time to listen to *The Shadow,* Titi." He turned the radio on and waited for it to warm up. And then he turned the dial pointer slowly as his father had taught him, and he worked it back and forth until he got the best reception on WEAF. Soon the radio was saying, "The makers of Blue Diamond Coal bring you — *The Shadow.*"

V

He had no coal.

He knew that it was better to buy anthracite than bituminous. Anthracite was hard coal, burned cleaner, gave off more heat. He could watch the delivery of anthracite to his building closely. He lived in apartment 2A, just over the *bodega,* and just over the cellar below the store. And directly under his Titi. On the sidewalk there was a round iron cover about 15 inches wide. A coal truck would back up to the sidewalk, and the driver would jump out and pull away the iron cover. Then he would drop a shining metal chute from the truck, align it into the hole, and jump back into the driver's seat and the truck lifted upward, sending the coal down the chute. When he was done the driver jumped into the tipped up back of the truck and swept down the chute any pieces of coal that remained. Then back on the sidewalk, he swept around the hole and replaced the iron cover. Sometimes the super would come out and sweep again.

The front of his building had a three part stoop: under his apartment was the *bodega.* In the center was the entrance to the building and on the other side was Suzi's Dry Cleaners. Beneath the *bodega,* was another flight of wooden steps laid over steel supports. He had been down to that basement once. It smelled terribly, was dark and dirty, and his father had been very angry, punishing him for going down there, making him kneel in one corner of their apartment for an hour. He had not gotten to see the coal bin. He had not gotten a piece of anthracite.

VI

"Sonny, it's very easy to do. You just grab the grey hair and pull it, that's all. Either with your fingers or with this."

"Doesn't it hurt?"

"No. It hurts more to have grey hair."

"I think it hurts."

"I'm telling you it doesn't hurt. It's my head and I ought to know. Now pull."

"Do I have to?"

"I'll pay you one penny for every one you pull. And I'll save the pennies here in this can. By the time a few years have passed you'll be rich."

"With all the money you owe me for the newspapers, too?"

"Yes, I'll put that in here too."

By the light of the window, next to the eight fish tanks, with the Spanish Hour playing on the radio, Sonny plucked his godmother's grey hairs. Through *tango* and *bolero*, he plucked away, disliking it very much. Sometimes he sang along with Libertad Lamarque, sometimes with Carlos Gardel, the two great singers the canaries were named after. He loved the tango that went:

La mujer que yo queria con todo mi corazon
Se me ha ido con el hombre que la supo seducir ...

He was not sure what the words meant.

"Titi, no more." He hated to pull them out, with or without the tweezer.

"Are you sure? You only took out ten."

"That's all I can find, I mean it."

"OK. Let's feed the fish and the canaries."

While Sonny went to the kitchen to get the fish food, Titi started moving the glass tops of the tanks in preparation.

"Which one goes in here?"

"Here give me that box. That's the special one. Look out, Oh God! It went out the window!!"

A guppy had leapt out of the tank and through the open window. When they looked out the window they couldn't see the fish.

Titi ran to the kitchen sink. "Take this glass of water, run down to the basement and look around for him. He might still be alive. He can't be on the sidewalk — he didn't jump that far out."

"Papi doesn't want me to go to the basement."

"Go on, this is an emergency. Get going."

Sonny ran out of the apartment and down the flight of steps, but his quick running was making him spill the water.

"Slow down a little — you need the water. And don't squeeze his body when you pick him up. Try to get him by the tail. Hurry up." Titi was yelling at the top of the stairs, and Beauty was barking, slipping and falling on the linoleum as she tried to make quick starts and tight turns, following Titi, who was running from the window to the hall, from the hall to the window. And the twelve canaries were all twittering in their four cages, making the cages swing, spilling water and Hartz Mountain seed all over the living room floor and onto the yoyo bedspread. The cages were hung in the bedroom doorway — the double doors long ago permanently pinned open by side tables.

By the time Sonny hit the street door he had about a half a glass of water, and he could hear his godmother yelling from the window "Hurry, hurry."

A few people had gathered on the sidewalk wondering who the lady in the 3rd floor window was yelling at. Sonny went down the stoop onto the sidewalk. He was concentrating on the glass of water, trying not to spill any more. He started down the stairs to the basement carefully, watching closely where he put his feet, in case the guppy was there. But then he saw the guppy lying on the next to the last wooden tread. He rushed down, gripped its tail and plunked it into the glass. The fish immediately began to swim.

He looked around for a piece of anthracite.

He saw none.

VII

When they had finished listening to the Great Gildersleeves, his godmother asked him to stay for a moment.

"Sonny, you know the little girl we call Tana, my godchild?"

"Yes, something happened to her mother."

"How do you know?"

"I heard Papi talking about it. Her mother jumped from the roof. Is it true?"

"That father of yours. How could he talk about such things to a child like you? Tana is coming to live here with me."

"Papi told me he was going to take me to the wake."

"He did! You are too young for a wake."

"Papi says I'm getting big now. That I have to learn about the world. That the world for a man is not these stories on the radio and singers like Carlos Gardel and Libertad Lamarque."

"Your father is wrong, Sonny. You're still little, and you have time to learn about the world — too much time. And I know more than your father — he thinks women don't know anything. Well, we work too, and hard, and we talk, and we live, and we know, we know more than the men, believe me Sonny. I am your second mother. You are my favorite godchild, more, you are my son. I sat here rocking you in the night, feeding you a bottle. When you were born, I was there, and I have seen you every day of your life — every single day. Where was your father? What does he know about anything? When Tana comes to live here nothing will change between us. You hear me? I will still be your second mother, and you will still be my son. Understand? Just because Tana comes here, doesn't mean anything will change between us. Now give me a kiss."

"*Bendición*, Titi."

"May God accompany you, and the Virgin favor you."

He did not immediately move feeling that something else had to happen. Although he had just been told that nothing would change he already felt a change.

Then his godmother added, "Don't forget to deliver the paper on Sunday."

VIII

Tana came to live at his godmother's house.

Tana was skinny and took hours to chew her food.

Tana took so long to eat, that they were late for the radio shows. The food on Tana's plate would get cold and grey and it looked like the food in Feeri's bowl.

And Tana's father came to visit every night. Tana's father was nice, and now he fed the fish in the ten tanks, and changed the paper bottoms of the six canary cages, and tuned the stations.

On Saturday night they listened to Judy Canova.

One Sunday morning when Sonny came to deliver the paper, it had already been delivered by Tana's father.

OSCAR'S STORY

Carlos and Sal had been drinking together off
and on, especially on weekends, for most of the
summer. Carlos was a junky Sal knew well, from
childhood, from before he had become a junky. And
he was the only junky Sal knew who liked both beer
and wine. But like other junkies, Carlos despised
rum and whiskey. If you just mentioned rum or
whiskey, Carlos would make a face, and then start
doing something with his throat and mouth that
seemed like he was having dry heaves. Seemed like,
because with Carlos you never knew. He had that
kind of sense of humor — the kind of humor
everybody had when they were all boys in junior
high school together.

One especially hot night, when beer or wine got
hot before you were even halfway through the can or
bottle, Carlos looked up after a long period of staring
into one blank space. Maybe it had been a reverie. It
came after he had stopped nodding — that amazing

balancing act that junkies do after they shoot heroin. They sway to one side, you swear they will fall, and tilted at some exaggerated angle, they suddenly pop upright, open their eyes a tiny bit only momentarily, and start tilting again at another angle. Swaying but not falling. You never saw one fall. You saw junkies all over Spanish Harlem nodding. Sometimes they would scratch some part of their body — usually the face, arms or legs. Lightly. In slow motion. Sometimes they scratched so hard you could see ulcerated skin suppurating and dried *cicatrices* on their arms or legs around the wrists or ankles. You also saw two guys dragging a third guy between them — keeping the third guy walking to prevent his slipping into a coma or stupor which was a way station not far from death, and therefore had to be avoided.

Sal never understood the whole sequence. Considering how many junkies he knew and how many he had seen, he had never spent one whole day with a junky. Sal didn't know what came first — a certain semi-consciousness followed by nodding and scratching — or the scratching first, then the other? You also never knew if the junkies weren't experimenting with whatever was cheap and available — catch of the day — and mixing heroin with amphetamines. The goof balls made them talk talk talk, the grass made them laugh, the heroin made them nod — and in combination, or washed down with beer or wine — what did that make them do? Maybe the scratching came as a sign that it was time for another dose.

Carlos stared at Sal, and then said, "My father used to say that thinking and reading too much was bad for the brain, you know? But I have met a lot of guys who thought a lot and a lot of guys who never thought about nothing, and their brains were the same. Did I ever tell you Oscar's story? I had a cousin named Oscar who played the drums, and went to the Bronx High School of Science, see. He was definitely the smartest guy in the whole family, but he wigged out, man. He went completely crazy. You know the Bronx High School of Science is one of the three greatest high schools in the United States? You knew that, right Sal? His father, who was my uncle and owned the candy store that used to be over there," — Carlos pointed to the southwest corner of Lexington Avenue and 110th Street — "it had the best malted milks in the whole neighborhood except for the ice cream parlor on 118th Street and Third Avenue, but you couldn't go up to 118th every day because of the Italians and especially the Italian gang called the Red Wings. My uncle used to put out that his son went crazy because he was so intelligent and he studied so hard. You know you gotta take a very tough test to get into Bronx Science — you know that, right Sal? But that was a whole lot of bullshit on my uncle's part. Oscar went crazy because his father, my uncle, Manolo, was a fucking tight wad. Hard as my elbow."

Carlos made a fist with his right hand and knocked on his left elbow for emphasis.

"Tacaño," he said in Spanish, then in case Sal hadn't understood, he used another Spanish word, *"maseta."* "Hard, hard, hard. Cheap. Chintzy."

Sal wondered what Chintzy had to do with Chintz. Maybe Chintz was a cheap cloth or fabric.

"Man, that cat was making big effing bucks from that candy store — he had the best collection of funny books, and I still remember the very clean tile floor, had a very pretty pattern in the center, dark tiles and light tiles, a border of black tiles, and a few red tiles forming a diamond here and there, and the tables was round pieces of marble, and the chairs was made out of bent wire, you remember, with wooden seats — they was like the side chairs in the barber shop too, and the same chairs they had on 118th. The joint always smelled great — it smelled a little like tobacco, a little like malt — a little like funny book paper — but Manolo wouldn't give his son a dime, not one tiny thin dime."

"When Oscar got a girlfriend the old man told Oscar to bring her to the candy store and he would sell her a soda or malted at a discount. Can you imagine that shit! A discount for his son's girlfriend! Then, when the girl got to the store, Manolo gave her the third degree. Man, it was an interrogation. Oscar wanted to die from embarrassment — his girl wanted to run and never see any of them again. But she was a sweet Puerto Rican girl, and she just sat answering Manolo's questions politely, never looking him in the eye. 'What does your father do? Does he work? Where? Does your mother work? Is she religious?'"

"But even after that, Manolo decided that his son was not studying enough and not practicing the drums enough. And he started saying that Oscar was sinful to go out with girls, that he ought to spend his full time studying and drumming."

"It was too much, man. One day I went in the candy store after school, and there was Oscar taking care of the counter, and doing drumming drills on his practice pad. You ever seen one of them things? It's a rubber thing, a hunk of rubber on a piece of wood, see. And the drum sticks bang bang on the rubber and they bounce back like off drum skins, but you ain't got the noise of drums, you know. My uncle, his father, was counting his money or some shit in the back. I know he wasn't stacking bottles, cause he had slave Oscar for all the real work. I said to Oscar, 'Man, what are you doing, two things at once!' Oscar said, 'Yeah, my father thinks I should practice when there are no customers.'"

"Then one day Manolo pulled the final drag. My uncle became a Pentecostal! A-le-lu-ji-ah! Oh man, I had to stop going to the candy store — the cat wouldn't stop talking — talking *El Señor,* talking God, talking Jesus the Man. Every time you went into the store he put the conversation into God. You said, 'How are you?' — he would say, 'Thanks to God, I'm OK. God is the source of our health.' And he would go into a preaching thing in a minute. Then he started having these preachers come in to break Oscar down, telling Oscar he was sinful cause he went out with girls and that he was sinful because he didn't obey his father and that he was sinful because he didn't practice enough and didn't study enough, and didn't want to turn his soul over to God, give his life to Jesus, or play the drums in the temple. See, they never say Church — they always say Temple."

"What I figured out from listening to Oscar was that these preacher cats had never seen no real sins so they thought all this bullshit was sins. I stopped going in the store. My cousin Oscar had become a maniac — he had a look in his eyes like Boris Karloff only Oscar wasn't acting. No matter how much I missed those malteds, or the egg creams, or the four-cent sodas — actually Pop's Candy Store on the other corner of Lexington Avenue made better egg creams, and also Pop, who wasn't a cheap skate, put more flavor in the four-cent sodas. When Pop made you a Lime Soda or a Cherry Lime Rickey, he let you see him putting the flavor in the seltzer, and his sodas was rich in taste, and they had strong color — my uncle Manolo he never let you see what he was doing behind the counter, and one of his four cent sodas looked like Dracula got to it first and drank all the blood out, the things looked anemic — if I went in the store and Manolo was there I would only buy a funny book. Then I would wait for my cousin to be taking care of the store to get my malteds. But even missing those malteds like I did — you know I think I had an addiction to them — it was too painful to go in the store. On this side you got preacher poppa nonstop. On this side you got Carlos, drumming drumming, his eyes looking wilder and wilder. Speaking less and less."

Carlos stopped talking. Sal drank wine and wondered what would happen next. Would Carlos continue the story, or would he start another story — forget that he had been telling a story? Or would the next part contradict everything Carlos had already said? You never knew, because you never knew what was talking — Carlos or the heroin, or Carlos and the heroin. Was it all made up? Was only part made up? Sal remembered the candy store, remembered the kid drumming on the pad.

"The summer came and went and Oscar was drumming all day and into the night. Then what had to happen happened. He wigged out."

"Oscar had been in the back busy bringing bottles from the basement, or to the basement, one, when he noticed that someone was calling him. That's when Manolo, his father, my uncle, that's his name, Manolo, when Manolo started yelling, 'Hey, Oscar what's taking you so long, are you drinking my sodas?' See, I happen to know that Oscar never drank sodas, never drank malteds. Oscar hated them, man, you know? The cigarettes was different. He'd cop a loosie once in a while, but he hated the sweet drinks. Oscar came out with a case of soda in his hand and put it down in the middle of the floor. Then he went over to his practice pad and took the drum sticks in his hands but he didn't play. He just sat over the practice pad. You ever seen a cat with distemper hanging over his water with a faraway look in his eyes? That's how Oscar was sitting. Manolo said, 'Jesus Sweet Love, what's wrong Oscar? Why aren't you practicing? Put that soda box where it belongs.' And Oscar got up from the counter, and started to gently drum on his father's head. Manolo started saying, 'Loco, Loco,' and started to back away. Manolo grabbed a broom and hit Oscar. And Oscar took the soda crate, one of them old ones that had wood and steel, and bashed his father over the head with it — and when his father was on the floor, bleeding from a gash on his bald skull, Oscar started drumming on his head again. Oscar's mother came in the store later, much later, late enough for the blood to be black and sticky on Manolo's head, black and sticky on the drum sticks — but Oscar was sitting right there next to his passed out father drumming drumming on his head. And when Oscar saw her he threw a bottle at her. Hit his mother right on the shoulder. She called the cops."

"I remember that kid, but I don't think I knew his name was Oscar," said Sal, paper wine cup in his hands. "I remember that kid sitting there drumming, drumming, drumming. I used to think of him as a lucky kid — all the new funny books, ice-cream, sodas — everything a kid could want, right?"

"Wrong," said Carlos, "wrong as shit. That kid, Oscar, never got the right time of day from his old man. I know, he was my cousin. I was better off than him — and I had nothing, not even a father."

"You know Carlos, I heard about the kid wigging out. But the story I got was that the kid had wigged out drumming and that a Pentecostal guy had cured the kid," said Sal, "cured the kid by bringing him Jesus, and that then the old man and old lady converted when they saw the miracle."

"Yeah, that's the story Manolo put out. But it wasn't like that — take it from me. I swear to God. I swear to my mother."

Carlos made the sign of the cross over himself. Then he put his right thumb over his right index finger's first joint, making a little cross, which he then kissed mentioning the Holy Ghost.

"I'm in the family — my mother still gets mail from my uncle Manolo. Manolo stood with a paralyzed face after that — either from the blood he lost, or the blow. You could see that he couldn't smile right on one side of his face, you know. And Oscar went to a funny farm, after they found him criminally insane — can you beat that shit? It was his father who was criminally insane."

"But anyway Oscar went upstate and he was doing good — he was like a trustee, you know, he worked with the gardeners cutting grass, trimming hedges, like that. And he never was interested in music. But every time his father or mother went to see him he would get all worked up again. Finally, they put a prohibition on the folks from visiting. So they checked out to P.R., man."

"That's a fucked-up story, isn't it?" asked Sal.

"No man, that ain't a fucked up story, it's just a story."

"Yeah? And where is that kid now — I mean Oscar, he's no kid anymore. Do you know?"

"Oscar? Oscar my cousin is still here, on our corner, because we are talking about him. He is alive with us. Give me some more wine."

Sal filled two more cups with the sweet "Sneaky Pete," no longer cold.

"I swear to my mother," said Carlos, then drank, as if it were a toast, "he's here on our corner."

Then he crossed his right thumb over the first joint of his right index finger and kissed it, and said, "May my mother drop dead if Oscar's not here on this corner with us."

SANTOS NEGRON

"No, you have it wrong — I want to play the 9 as the first number — if it doesn't come out, then I want to play two dollars on it as the second number, and if it doesn't come out second, I want to play it for the last number for three dollars."

"Hey — what do you do — stay up all night to invent these complicated bets?"

"Just take my bets — I'm late for work." Santos Negron turned and walked out of the *botánica* briskly toward the subway on 103rd Street and Lexington. He hated to talk to the number collector, and he hated the *botánica,* with its stink of incense and its confusion of catholic saints, spiritism, witchcraft and *santeria.* Plaster saints next to desiccated sea horses, rosaries next to rancid potions. Pray with one, bathe with the other. They might change your luck.

Chin was setting up his boxes of mangoes and tropical vegetables as he did every weekday morning, hanging his scale on the support rod of the Walk/Don't-Walk traffic sign.

"Buenos dias, Chin."

"Buenos dias, Santos."

He entered the stairwell of the subway and was repelled by the overpowering urine smell. Every morning it was like stepping into a giant *palangana,* walking through the chamber pot on the way to the train.

Every morning it was the same sequence — the *botánica,* Chin, the urine-well.

Santos changed trains at 59th Street and one stop later emerged from the subway right under the hotel where he worked. He took out one of his Lucky Strikes and puffed in relaxation watching the people walking on Fifth Avenue, hurrying to work. He enjoyed these twenty minutes every morning. They gave him an opportunity to gather up all his cares, to savor his morning cigarette, his morning relationship to all these people.

Then Pedro came, waved to him, and together in silence they went down to the basement of the Hotel Plaza, where the laundry was. Pedro was a presser, and Santos sometimes a floorman, most times a bin and sheet man. They changed into their white work uniforms in silence. Pedro was mute, but his muteness had not prevented them from forming a deep friendship.

Twice a week Santos would visit Pedro at home, timing his visits to arrive well after dinner. Pedro's wife Anita would say, "Santos, why didn't you come earlier and have dinner with us?" and he would always answer, "I forget to come earlier, that's all — do you have any coffee left?" Anita never had coffee left — she always boiled up a new pot full and strained it through the flannel. It was the only way to make coffee as far as she was concerned. And Santos agreed. They would talk about world politics and Santos would play with the children. After an hour and a half Santos would leave — feeling warm and fulfilled. He was godfather to Pedro Jr., and that was his closest connection to a family.

II

"How can you believe that if I hit it on the first, I would still play it again for the second and third? What do you think I am — crazy?"

"You don't make your bets clear, that's not my problem. Pain in the ass anyway — all you play is the single numbers."

"You don't like that because I hit you too often, don't I?"

"Maybe you'd like to find another place to play your numbers — I don't need your business."

"Yeah — what a good idea. That's one thing I can find, thousands of cheap number collectors like you."

He turned out and walked past the plaster Indian bust with the *santeria* collar on it, next to the large candle that said, "change your luck."

"*Buenos dias,* Chin."

"*Buenos dias,* Santos."

Urine well.

Change on 59th Street.

Puff on a Lucky Strike.

Going to change number collectors and tonight, instead of walking home along Madison Avenue looking in the store windows, he was going to take the subway home and knock on Elena's door and make her his business proposition.

Pedro arrived and they went down to the laundry, into the white uniform. Mrs. Tolliver, his boss, told him she wanted him in the bin today. The bin was the bottom of all the laundry chutes in the Hotel Plaza. Maids tore down the rooms and placed the soiled linens in a bag on their carts. The floorman took the linens from their carts and put them in his tub, and when his tub was full, he emptied it into the chutes that opened on each floor. Down the chutes the dirty sheets, towels, face cloths, shoe shine rags, pillow cases, table cloths and napkins, went tumbling until they hit the bottom. There, under the weight of the succeeding loads they jammed up the chute openings into the "bin."

A crew of five men worked feverishly, to unstop the chutes and at the same time to sort the linen into carts that carried away just sheets, or just pillow cases, or just towels. The men worked seriously on the platform, where because heat rises, all the hot air of the giant washing machines, giant drying machines, and giant pressing machines, accumulated. The weight of the compressed linen had the potential force of slapping a man flat against a wall, if he wasn't nimble when he opened a stoppered chute. But they had learned to talk and do their work. And the danger from the chutes was generally over by 11:30 a.m., and then only the sorting was left to do. Smelly work the sorting, for the linen came down with all kinds of civilized and uncivilized objects, food and puke, semen and blood.

Elpidio, the man from the Lower East Side, who was the best travelled and was perhaps the best read among them, was saying that man's fecal matter was the stinkiest in the world.

Willie laughed, said, "You have smelled all the shit in the world, Elpidio?"

"You see," said Elpidio, "you will always be ignorant, because you'd rather laugh than think."

"Hey, shit expert, remember you're just a laundry worker like I am. Or is this the air conditioned part of the University?"

Elpidio ignored Willie, turning to Santos. "What do you think, Santos?"

"I think you'd better pull the #3 chute, and I think you're wrong. There's no such thing as bad smells or good smells, bad words or good words, ugly days or pretty days. A certain rainy day can be more beautiful than an ordinary sunny day. Some people like Old Spice and some like Prince George. Some people like the smell of cigars, others get sick on them."

"Attaboy, Santos," said Willie, "now I got two professors of shit philosophy. You guys think you could help me get my high school diploma?"

"I think Santos is right," said Angel. "In Hawaii they eat a fish sauce which is practically rotten, in

Japan raw fish, in Africa ants and grasshoppers, in France brains with eggs and frogs legs."

The lunch bell rang.

Willie said, "I think it's jerks like us in the farthole of this city who think the cow manure is sweet to the farmer. The farmer hates the cows, hates the cow manure, hates the weather. Only us city jerks think a farm is heaven. I seen the farmer punch the cows — that's right, my uncle took his big fist and slammed it into a cow that wouldn't move." They were all jogging down the stairs of the bin, down the main laundry floor, down to the bathroom to wash up and run out and get a quick lunch. The married men had their lunch buckets or *friambreras*, or brown bags, and sat in the locker room, and some played dominoes and some played 500 rummy. Santos went out to lunch with Nelson. Nelson was the man who put large armfuls of wet wash into the drying machine, and everyday for lunch during the season only ate a basket of strawberries.

III

"I want to play the 0 and the 3 with two dollars for first, then either the 0 or the 3 if one comes out first, you understand, and then the 0 and the 3 for last for two dollars if neither has still come out; okay?"

"Yeah, I got it. What else?"

"Nothing for today, thank you."

The new betting parlor was a combination *botánica* and flower shop. As fronts they seemed incredibly naive to Santos Negron. "If I were a cop, I would bust ten of these a day." But when he told that to Elpidio, in the bin, Elpidio said, "No you wouldn't, because each place would give you five dollars a day and each day you would keep forty dollars and give your sergeant ten dollars, and he would give the captain five dollars, and you wouldn't bust anybody but the teenagers and the junkies who wouldn't know about paying or couldn't pay."

Elpidio was a man you could talk to because he knew a lot. He should describe his plan to Elpidio and see what he thought of it. Now that his courage had failed and he had not knocked at Elena's door, he had an opportunity to test his idea. Perhaps his failure of courage had spared him from making a fool of himself. What if Elena found the whole idea stupid?

"*Buenos dias,* Santos."

He had almost walked past Chin without greeting him.

"*Buenos dias,* Chin."

Chamber pot.

59th Street.

Lucky Strike.

White suit.

Mrs. Tolliver needed Santos on the floor today because one of the floormen was out. Santos had to go back and get into his special white uniform of the floorman and headed up to the floors assigned to him. He didn't mind doing the floor work — and it was a hell of a lot cooler on the floors than in the laundry — but at the same time you had to hurry more and the maids were always yelling at you to empty their carts. But his principal reason for not liking the floors was that he noticed, and the other men agreed, that they only put white men to work on the floors, and the only time anybody as dark-skinned as Santos was allowed up there was when someone was absent and Santos was the only remedy.

When noontime came he decided not to go to lunch, because he was so behind in his work. He knew that if he was behind, then the men below in the bin would also be behind and that everyone would be annoyed, including Mrs. Tolliver.

At 1:00 p.m. he had caught up and came down to lunch, but Mrs. Tolliver wanted to see him.

"Why did you get so far behind, Santos?"

"Mrs. Tolliver — you know I started forty-five minutes later than the floorman. Then the maids don't let you get organized. They are yelling at me, 'Do me, do me, do me.' I can't do everybody at one time. That's all."

"Santos, do you like the job of floorman?"

"It's okay."

"If this fellow is absent once more, I'm going to give you the job permanently. Would you like that?"

"Not really, Mrs. Tolliver. I'm glad you think about me, but I'd rather stay down here where all my friends are. It's the same money."

"Would you do it for a raise?"

"No. I'm sorry I mentioned the money. I'll stay down here with my friends, Mrs. Tolliver, and once in a while I'll help you out and go upstairs."

"Okay, Santos, take your lunch hour now and bring me your time card so I can initial it for you."

In the afternoon Santos couldn't get close enough to Elpidio to talk, but Willie was furious with him. "You dope, you passed up a promotion — maybe a raise. You know the job up there is easier. You wear a nicer uniform, you can fool around with the maids — it's cool up there. That's why we Puerto Ricans won't make it in this town. We're too goddamned sentimental. You'd rather stay down here talking about cow manure. You know from a job up there you could become a houseman or something better. Work less, make more, man. That's how it's supposed to be, Santos."

"Willie, you know what? I'm going to ask Mrs. Tolliver to let me train you. The next time I go up to do floorman I'll take you, and then after that you'll get the promotion, Willie. You deserve it, you're a young guy with a family — anyway, I'm going into business for myself."

"Oh, yeah? What kinda business, Santos?"

"I'm going to make money in the park on weekends, Willie — selling food and beer and soda to the ball players on Saturdays and Sundays."

"Hey, Santos, what a good idea — what the hell — you don't do nothing on the weekends anyway, right?"

"Right, and you know I'm a good cook, and you don't need to be a bartender to sell beer."

"Santos, here comes Mrs. Tolliver."

"Boys, I don't mind you talking, but I don't think you're moving those sheets fast enough."

"Mrs. Tolliver, you know what we were talking about? I think Willie would make a good floorman. Why don't you let me take him up with me when I go again? What do you say, Mrs. Tolliver?"

"I say, I'll think about it, Santos. Meanwhile how about moving those sheets faster?"

IV

"You made twenty-four dollars yesterday. The 0 was first and 3 second. What do you like for today?"

"Today I want to play the 2, that's all. Two dollars each time."

"No split bets today?"

"No, thanks."

As he turned to go out of the store he saw a small bottle that said "Courage." He took it and went back to the window. "How much?" "Sixty-five cents." He paid the man and pocketed the bottle for reading on the subway. Down the block he could see Chin laying out boxes of avocados and also yams and *yuca;* and Santos wondered why Chin could do it and he couldn't. You just had to go out there, hang your scale and start. What was so hard about it?

"Buenos dias, Chin."

"Buenos dias, Santos."

Palangana.

59th Street.

Lucky Struck.

That night he rode the train home. He had thrown the bottle away without reading its label. He had determined that if Chin could do it, so could he — he didn't need any of that *hechiceria* in bottles to have courage.

He knocked on Elena's door.

He said, "Me, Santos."

"Santos?" she said, opening the door.

"Yes, Santos," he said, too loudly he felt, and now his heart was beating very fast.

Elena was standing in the doorway not very sure of what to do. She had known this man for many years, but he had never knocked at her door before.

"Are you all right?" she asked after a while.

"Yes, may I come in? I want to talk to you."

"Yes, come in, sit down."

The apartment door opened into the kitchen. He took a chair at the table. He was too embarrassed to enter the living room.

"Well, I meant in the living room," she said, feeling like a bad hostess.

"I need to talk to you."

"So you already said."

"Well, sit down then. I can't talk while you are standing."

Elena was taken aback by his abruptness, but still thought it had to do with herself, who was not making him feel comfortable.

"Would you like a beer?"

"Yes, thank you."

Elena opened the refrigerator and removed two bottles of Miller beer. Santos hated Miller beer and immediately tried to think up a reason for not drinking it — but there were no reasons, so he drank it. He looked around and realized that Elena was neat as a pin.

"I came to make you a business proposition, Elena. I have an idea for a business, but I need a partner. I know you're a good cook, and I'm a cook myself."

"Oh — now I know why you never buy my food."

"That's right, I cook for myself quite well."

"And how do you know I'm a good cook?" Elena was drinking her beer out of a glass.

Now that Santos was talking — he had finally done it — he felt very powerful, and very relaxed. He liked the way Elena had pulled her hair straight back on her head and made a bun in the back. She looked beautiful, like a mature woman who broached no nonsense, and was not tying her hair into rollers, or cutting it into hair shapes more appropriate for teenagers. And she was a slim woman, in fact, even sinewy, and he liked that, too — the body of an athlete, only not from sports, but from hard work and a hard life. Even the beer tasted good.

"Because the other men tell me. And so does my compadre — I'm Pedro's son's godfather — he used to buy food from you years ago."

"The deaf-mute guy?"

"Only mute, not deaf."

"He got married — that's how I lose all my customers."

"Look, Elena, here's my idea. I go to the park a lot on Saturdays and Sundays. From early in the morning to sunset there are hundreds of Puerto Rican ball players with their wives and their kids in the park. Softball players and baseball players. They need food and they need drinks. Right now they bring stuff from home, mostly sandwiches because the wives don't want to cook and because rice and beans cold is terrible."

"I think if I go to the park every Saturday and Sunday and cook fresh food and sell cold beer and soda, I'll make money. But it's too much for one person, so I need a partner. And I might as well have a partner that can cook. What do you say?"

Now that he had gotten it all out, his enthusiasm for an idea that had been brewing since the previous summer was waning. She was probably going to laugh.

But Elena did not laugh. She looked closely at him and got up and went to the refrigerator for another two beers.

"And what do I have to do?"

"Just help me plan. Help me do the whole thing. I cook for myself, but I don't really know how to cook for a hundred. Do you?"

"No." Elena answered quickly because in her wildest dreams she had never had one hundred customers. The men who purchased food from her on a weekly plan and the few families who occasionally purchased meals had never numbered more than twenty.

"Twenty is the most I ever cooked for. Look at my kitchen, I don't even have a large pot. Sometimes I have four pots going, one on each burner."

"Well, that's the kind of help I need."

"Do I have to put up money?"

"No, I'll put up all the money."

"And how do we split the profits?"

"As soon as I take out what I put up at first, we go fifty-fifty."

She thought about his offer. He didn't really need a partner.

"You don't really need a partner. All you need is an employee to help you."

"Oh no. This business has to be done as a partnership. Two people who are interested in the business. Two people who know how to cook and want to make tasty foods. That's what's going to make it a success."

"When do you want to start?"

"This Saturday. I get paid Friday. We can pick out all the things we need and Friday I'll pay for them. We'll be in the park on Saturday at 10:00 a.m. and by 12:00 we start making money."

"How much do you think we're going to make?"

"How much do you think is worth your while?"

"I don't know," said Elena, "I really don't know. I'm not making anything Saturdays now — I guess if I made anything, I'd be okay."

"That's how I feel. I go to the park on the weekends anyway. But I think after we pay our bills, we could make sixty dollars each and every weekend."

"Sixty dollars!"

"That's what I said, sixty dollars each! Sixty dollars a day!"

Santos lit a Lucky Strike, they each had their private thoughts, and then started planning.

V

"I want to play the 1, 2, 3, in first, second, and third, with one, two, and three dollars; you understand?"

"Yeah — what else?"

"I want a bottle of 'luck', and do you know anything about what's good when you're going to start a new business?"

"Sixty-five for the small bottle of luck. The one who knows all about that stuff doesn't come in until 11 o'clock in the morning."

"Look, could you find out for me and I'll buy it from you tomorrow?

"Sure."

He liked the man at this betting parlor. He was very business-like and never commented on Santos' bets.

"*Buenos dias,* Chin."

"*Buenos dias,* Santos."

Chamber Pot.

59th Street.

Lucky Strike.

Chin does well, I see empty boxes in the evening. Pedro arrived and they went down to the laundry's dressing room, and he told Pedro, "I'll be at your house tonight."

Mrs. Tolliver needed him on the floors, but wouldn't send Willie because Elpidio was also out. He started about forty-five minutes later than the regular floorman, and when he hit the top floor of his assigned floors the maids were furious. "Do me, Do me," they were all yelling. Every room in the hotel was occupied and they were all trying to keep up with their own time schedules. Santos literally ran up and down the halls wildly pushing the tub over the carpeted floors.

When he came down at 1:15, Mrs. Tolliver said, "Pretty good, Santos, but now I need you in the bin — they are way behind up there — don't even change your uniform."

Willie was moving his arms like a windmill, throwing sheets, pillow cases, table cloths at a furious rate. Santos had never seen Willie work like that. Had never seen anybody work like that in the bin. What a difference two men made.

Santos ripped into the pile, trying to work a steady rhythm, but he could see that they were at about 10:30's load — or more than two hours behind.

"What happened Willie, we shouldn't be so far behind?"

"Yeah, but Nelson came in late of all days. And the shit philosopher must be out in the fields today. But now that you're here we'll knock this crap out in an hour — what do you say?"

They turned to the piles of laundry and sorted and threw in silence with a great concentration. When the load was like this you could not talk. Talk was not conducive to this rhythm of work. But work like this was good for thinking.

"Stand clear," shouted Willie, "I'm going to open this chute."

But Willie couldn't budge the chute. With the shortage of workers one chute hadn't been unstopped the whole day.

"Santos, you're stronger than me — clear this chute and I'll go on in the pile."

Santos went to the chute and Willie went back to the pile starting in faster than he'd been going before.

Santos told him, "Steady, Willie, it's more important to work steady than to go too fast. We'll finish today by six."

"Yeah," said Willie, "but what about Nelson? If he doesn't get his strawberries soon, he's gonna have withdrawal symptoms."

They all laughed and Santos kept tugging at the chute. "Hey fellas, stand clear. When this hole opens, it's going to be like a tidal wave." But when he opened it, Nelson was moving across the bin and the stream of fast moving heavy linens hit him and knocked him over the rail of the bin into one of the tubs below. They all saw it, but couldn't do anything about it. Nelson opened a small cut on his left arm, but was otherwise unhurt. He had cut himself on one of the metal bars that made up the super-structure of the tub.

Mrs. Tolliver told them to stop. "It's time you took your lunch break. We're way behind anyway and I don't want any more accidents."

They worked late that night and Santos went straight home instead of going to Pedro's. When he was going up the stairs, Elena opened her door and asked, "Can I talk to you?"

"Sure." Even though he was quite tired, he could not say no to his partner.

Elena saw to it that he sat in the living room. And tonight she had Schaefer beer instead of Millers. And he noticed again how neat everything was — the linoleum on the floor sparkled.

Elena said, "Santos, I'm worried. What if you put up everything and it doesn't work? Maria was telling me that cooking over charcoals is very different from the top of the stove. We could get smokey rice and things like that."

"Today I saw a man hit by a thousand pounds of laundry going about thirty miles an hour. He was knocked over a rail and fell about eight feet. But he fell into a bunch of sheets, and all he did was get a little bandaid cut on his arm. If it doesn't come out right, it doesn't matter. I told you I go to the park every weekend anyway. As for the money, I'll just make believe I lost it in the numbers, that's all."

And somehow they wound up in bed that night, and Elena was good, and Santos was good.

VI

"You know you're a lucky fellow. You don't need this bottle of luck. You hit all the numbers yesterday, 1,2,3. Here, you made $48 yesterday. Why don't you play the whole number? You could have made a couple of thousand yesterday."

"I knew they were gonna come out. Today I play 7's one dollar each. My motto is, 'Have no greed.'

See, I believe that if you want to win too badly, you lose — to win you have to be indifferent."

There was no Chin and no chamber pot and no 59th Street because today was Saturday. Smoke a Lucky Strike outside the *botánica* and stare in its window at all the foolishness — St. Anthony and St. Barbara, the candles and the rosary. If things go well today and tomorrow, I will buy a pretty rosary for Elena.

By 10:30 a.m. they were in the park and the fire was lit. Santos had taken a supermarket cart and modified it so that it carried everything they needed. It was quite heavy, and he had already decided that he needed another kind of vehicle, or perhaps two vehicles. And the day went well. Willie and Nelson and Elpidio and Pedro and his wife all came and ate and drank beer. And the ball players and their wives enjoyed the food and complimented the cook on the rice and beans and the fresh fried chicken, and by a quarter of three they had sold out everything they had and everyone had had a great time. And they knew they would need two carts by next Saturday.

And when they were in Elena's kitchen washing the pots and utensils and Santos was drinking a Budweiser beer, Elena asked him, "Is it true that you tried to kill Chin once?" And Santos took a quick drink from his beer and looked at her and said, "The other way around," and he drank more beer. And Elena said, "He is considered a very dangerous man, but you have the reputation of having beaten him."

Santos laughed and was pleased. And he realized now why everyone on the block was both distant and deferential. Chin was a two time loser — a convict whom everyone had feared, but whose last time in jail had broken him.

"Listen," said Santos drinking more beer, "Chin used to be frightening — now he's just a hard-working vegetable seller. He doesn't scare anybody any more."

"Well is it true that you almost killed him?"

"No. He tried to kill me. Chin was the best pool player in the neighborhood. In those days there was a pool room on Lexington Avenue between 108th and 109th Streets. One day Chin challenged me to a game. I was no match for him — so he started to play with one hand. I was still no match for him. He was winning all the way easily. I decided to make a shot that depended on a very thin cut. Chin said to me, 'You think you're going to make that cut?' I told him, 'I'm losing anyway, so I'm going to enjoy my game. I'm going to cut this so thin you'll think I did it with a razor blade instead of a cue stick.'"

"Chin bet me $10 I wouldn't do it. I took the bet because I have always calculated my luck very well. I cut the ball even finer than I expected. And Chin was furious. He said he wouldn't pay. I told him I was going to break the pool stick over his head. He took out a knife and charged at me. It wasn't the ten bucks — he was just furious that an amateur like me had made such an impossible shot. I took the knife from him, but I was cut. Here, see it? I started beating Chin with my cue stick, but somebody called the police. When they came, I had the knife and was bleeding. The cops wanted to know what happened. I told them that I had cut myself accidentally with my own knife. They didn't believe it, but what could they do. Nobody else would talk. Everybody in the pool room claimed they were busy playing. So the cops left. And Chin looked at me and I looked at Chin, and I gave him back his knife. And he said, '*Buenos dias,* Santos,' and I said, '*Buenos dias,* Chin.'"

Later she said to him, "Chin was my boyfriend once; does it bother you?"

And later she said to him, "We did well today, we're going to make $50 a day each. That's very good money."

And much later they were in bed, and Elena was good, and Santos was good.

"AGUA VIVA,"
A SCULPTURE BY
ALFREDO GONZALEZ

The knuckles ached as did the hands of the man who had been dragging chain and handling heavy iron pieces for years. His greasy hands, hair follicles and pores super-saturated with oils, grime and ferrous particles caught and caked in them, no longer felt the long, sharp, and shallow cuts, or the multiple punctures that scalpeled edges on cams and cogs of highly polished steel and burrs on poorly finished cast iron inflict on human skin.

He had never liked work gloves.

He had not washed his hands for five years.

He tugged at the tangle of chains, of pulleys, of polished parts, of alternately painted and rusty parts that lay scrambled on the concrete driveway next to his house and midway between the street and his garage. He was pulling the mass toward the garage when it occurred to him that it would make a very beautiful sculpture. He would have to affix one end to the top of an A-frame, arrange the chains like runners of Virginia Creeper and then tie weights at the bottom of each of the chains so that they would hang taut. He could call it *Agua Viva* because it would remind him of the jellyfish that inhabit the waters off Puerto Rico.

There was a good A-frame in the shed. Too good in fact. He would have to cover part of the frame under plastic while he hosed the A-frame down to induce some rust, and he would probably have to distress the A-frame with the peen side of one of his hammers to chip away the industrially baked-on enamel paint.

You had to transform the A-frame to make the whole piece harmonious. Otherwise it would be two separate elements — one of pretty painted parts and one of junk. The A-frame had to be distressed, yes. Distress can turn the dull to beauty.

Iron and steel do not tangle like thread, cord or rope. Perhaps chain tangles like logs, and words like jam or snag would be better to describe what happens when links twist out of line and chains of different gauge twine like tresses. Wood has water, or better said, logs have water to propel them part of their way. Professional handlers have winches and pulleys and special vehicles to transport piles like the one the man now dragged up the slightly inclining driveway.

Something hit his face, and he realized that something had hit his body twice before. He looked up to see three boys throwing things at him that he could not immediately identify. Nor could he recognize the boys. Were they his son's friends? Where was his son?

"Filthy Fredo, filthy Fredo, ya ya ya-ya-ya," they shouted.

Were they talking to him? Who was "filthy Fredo"? He dropped the mass of chains and took up one of the thrown things. It was a clod of soil with tufts of grass and grass roots holding it together.

"Dirt for the dirty, dirt for the dirty, filth for filthy Fredo," chanted the boys, nearby.

In his hand the sod felt like a pearl compared to the usual objects he handled. He threw it and hit one of the boys squarely on the face, striking both the nose and lips. The boy, perhaps eleven, started to cry and bleed at the same time. None ran. The man started forward and the boy, perhaps fourteen years old, decided to run. But the man caught him and clamped one hand on the boy's shoulder at the same time that he brought his other hand open across the boy's head. With a dull "whup," the boy twirled, and the man then shove-kicked the boy down the driveway. The third boy, the youngest of all, was long ago gone.

From across the street a man hollered "Good for you Gonzalez. Welcome back to earth."

What the man across the street knew, and the boys had known, was that the man they all called "filthy Fredo" had never retaliated, had never even chased the taunting teenagers or the ya-ya-yaing younger boys. No wonder they were caught off guard. In fact, before this moment he had never reacted at all, not for five and maybe seven years.

To anything.

Except iron and steel.

Wheels and manhole covers, and grates and wrenches and gaggers and rods and gears, and discs and platens and gates, and chucks and clutches and grills, and spools and bobbins, locks and keys, pinions and racks and gaffles, and meat-hooks and ball-joints and shuttles and flycocks and gaffers, and dividers and rasps, and gyroscopes, graters, and gymbals, grab-hooks, and a thousand parts too small or too complex or too divorced from their origin or context or too specialized and thus identifiable only by their creator, cluttered the length and breadth of the walls of his house, of the walls of his garage, of the walls of his shed, and finally, having displaced length and breadth, the pieces also piled and accumulated in corners and centers, so that finally, finally, they even displaced the girth, the very girth of his abode.

His house had become the lair of the iron woodchuck, the hive of the iron bee, the storeroom of the iron squirrel, the complex of chambers of the iron ant.

From wall to wall, from floor to ceiling the mountain of metal was broken only by a thin corridor that was wide enough for the passage of one man at a time and which changed direction as often as a young river in the mountain.

In the beginning — not in the very beginning of his life when he was named Alfredo after months and months of arguing between his mother and father. In that beginning he had been the first son, and his parents had spent a considerable amount of their waking hours, perhaps of their sleeping hours also, in consideration of an appropriate name. By the seventh child, selecting names was less of a problem. In the beginning, "Alfredo" had been agreed to after eight and one half months of arguing, and just fourteen hours before he was born. As soon as he was brought home, his father looked at him all swaddled against the winter and said, "If we were still in Puerto Rico, he would not wear so much clothing, and oddly, I would find him bigger. Now he looks so small that I, I think I shall call him Fredo."

The boys were cruel and called him filthy Fredo, thus facing a creature they only partly recognized and did not understand. The scientists created chains of -*noias* and -*phrenias* and complicated sprockets of interlocking phrases to describe Fredo. In the end — after a year — they released him as "traumatized" but "harmless," and on the cover of the file folder that contained his dossier there was a number, a date, and the simple phrase "returned to community." There was no name on the face of the folder, but perhaps the letters GON were an abbreviation for "Gonzalez" rather than an abbreviation for "Gone."

But in the beginning of the iron collecting, he had brought the pieces home after much thinking, hesitation, selection and bartering. Then he would spend hours removing paint or rust, applying naval jelly or a torch and wire brush depending on the need. And he would hang the pieces, leaving "air" around each piece so that it could "breathe" and be seen both in the beauty of its form, composition and harmony, its exquisite proportions, or in its indivisible simplicity, in its own beauty, and in relation to the other members of the displayed collection. And he kept notebooks, assigning a number, noting measurements, weights, a description of the object, what metal it was, its uses or purpose, if he knew it, and its provenance, if he knew that. A price and date would be entered if it was a purchase, and if it had been found or given to him, the place found, or the name of the giver. Finally, if any appeared, the maker's mark, and if known, who that mark belonged to. There generally was a drawing or a photograph as well.

Thus in the beginning, the interest in collecting had been a pleasure and a hobby and even a science — sometimes the avid amateur can be more thorough than the museum professional. And the iron had occupied a portion of his life space, his time, his psyche, his physical space. Now it was iron and steel wall to wall — one of a kind decaying next to scrap, art under decoration under function under technology under dross, all in an incubator — no, a compost. And parallel to this total displacement of his physical space iron had totally replaced his time or blocked or separated him from time. As if time in it's rigid tick tock trajectory were thwarted by the crumpled metallic maze. Or perhaps the magnetic mass was so great it created a false true north for time. Or perhaps time entering the irrational dimension of this prodigious pile was bent the way sun rays refract through angled glass and then cannot escape the greenhouse.

Alfredo Gonzalez, mostly known as Fredo, also known as "filthy Fredo" entered his house and was shocked at the disorder. It was as if he had entered a tight stack section of a library with a minimum walk space between the stacks. But there were neither books nor shelves, just piles of metal objects — from clockworks to the flywheel of a tractor, to the cap piece of a massive boiler. There was barely a path among the piles of objects. He switched on a lamp that was made from a cast-iron newel post that he had assembled in 1959, but it would not light. Neither would any others when he could reach around the mountains of objects to try switches.

Had it not been for the newel post he would not have believed he was in his own home.

He worked his way to the telephone, which buried under dirt and grease, did not work. Neither was there water or gas in the kitchen and the windows were opaque. The meager grey light that filtered through was further defeated by the piles and piles of objects on the available counter space and leaning in rows against the cabinets on the floors. He could not locate the refrigerator.

He remembered that his hallway bathroom had two windows. But even there the light was insufficient to illuminate his image in the mirror. He opened one half of one window with a small pry bar that lay behind the commode. And he turned and gazed in the mirror — what he saw there stopped his heart.

In the mirror was the head and shoulders of a man who had not bathed, shaven, or shorn his hair for five or more years and who had not seen himself in that time either.

He reacted by looking at his hands, one of which still held the pry bar. In disbelief, he raised his hands and looked again in the mirror. The hands matched, and then there was an explosion. The hand holding the pry bar had come down on the mirror creating everything from glass dust to splinters to large chunks which still held the bizarre face.

Fredo gasped, and his breath came short and with difficulty, as if he had been running. His head whirled with fear, with incomprehension with loathing with disorientation with dread. He was about to pass out when he saw the figure of the teenage boy go up the driveway.

The boy was spraying gasoline over the shed, the garage, and even on the pile of chains still at the upper end of the driveway as Fredo came around the house. When the boy saw filthy Fredo he panicked and quickly lit the book of matches which at once ignited the boy's hands and one of his trouser legs.

Fredo pushed the boy down to the ground and away from the gasoline. He was less concerned with the boy than with keeping the gasoline from igniting, although when he contemplated the shed and garage they were crammed solid containers of spare parts with very little to burn — a bit of residue of grease or oil. The structures themselves were of wood as one would expect from a man who loved iron and would have nothing but contempt for aluminum siding or pre-fab metal panels. He remembered now that he had read in one of his books on iron:

One would expect to find few samples of ancient iron works, and many of brass and bronze. However the reverse is true, for nothing is as destructive as man, and while time has a ferocious effect on badly cured and maintained forged or cast iron, man has an even more pernicious effect on brass and bronze. Because they are more precious and often employed by men of war, ornate baptistry doors and colossal cannons are subject to remelting and reworking. Works of art become works of war, in turn plain shields are converted to decorative serving platters. Iron, properly forged and cured, watches implacably resisting wave after wave of heat and cold, army after army.

The neighbor from across the street was spraying the boy on the ground with a huge fire extinguisher. "Serves 'm right," the neighbor was saying, then turning his extinguisher onto the non-burning gasoline and the yet to be assembled sculpture called "*Agua Viva*" and winking "just in case, you never know." He seemed to be enjoying the steady rope of white foam uncoiling from the extinguisher.

"What do you want to do with this boy?"

Fredo wanted to say "nothing" but no sound came from him. When he tried again a very guttural noise that sounded like "teen" came out.

He had not spoken in over five years.

"Nothing? You wanna do nothing?"

Fredo shook his head yes.

The neighbor helped the boy up and said to him, "Don't ever come in this block again and I won't tell your father the details of this accident. Let's just say one of your jerky friends sprayed you with a fire extinguisher after you lit up a can of lighter fluid. And for god's sake leave this man alone."

"Tell me Fredo, have you looked at yourself in a mirror today? Because you are not the man in the mirror. I know you Fredo — come over to my house I'll give you a haircut, a shave, a cold beer, you can take a bath — two baths, and I'll tell you what I think happened to you. Do you hear me Fredo? Do you understand?"

Fredo shook his head and made a sound like a hack saw on cast iron. It was "yes."

OTHER LATINO TITLES
AVAILABLE FROM CURBSTONE PRESS

MIRRORS BENEATH THE EARTH
Short Fiction by Chicano Writers
edited by Ray González

"As I read the stories, I was in a universe without dividing
lines, without borders. Read and see and hear for yourself
how they open and describe worlds heretofore banned and
ignored...and how rich and substantial American literature
becomes by their inclusion." — Jimmy Santiago Baca
$13.95 paper, 1-880684-02-0

ALWAYS RUNNING
La Vida Loca: Gang Days in L.A.
by Luis J. Rodriguez

"A permanent testament to human courage and transcend-
ence. And what a great story it tells." — Jonathan Kozol
"Bravo, Luis J. Rodríguez, for the beauty of a strong, singular
voice.... Must reading. Punto!!" — Piri Thomas
$19.95 cloth, 1-880684-06-3

REBELLION IS THE CIRCLE OF A LOVER'S HANDS
a bilingual edition of poetry by Martín Espada
translated by the author and Camilo Pérez-Bustillo

About this powerful collection of poems, which received the
1989 PEN/Revson Award for poetry, the judges (Carolyn
Forché, Daniel Halpern & Charles Simic) said: "Whoever in
the future wishes to find out the truth about our age will have
to read poets like Martín Espada."
$9.95 paper, 0-915306-95-6

FOR A CATALOG, SEND YOUR REQUEST TO:
Curbstone Press, 321 Jackson Street, Willimantic, CT 06226